DEATH ON THE QUAI

A Paris Booksellers Mystery

EVAN HIRST

ABOUT THE AUTHOR

Spurred on by a passion for history and a love of adventure,

Evan Hirst has lived and worked all over the world and now

lives in Paris.

Evan's Paris Booksellers Mysteries plunge into the joys and

tribulations of living in Paris, where food, wine and crime

make life worth living... along with a book or two.

Books in the series are stand-alones and can be read in any order.

Book 1: Death on the Seine
Book 2: Death in the Louvre
Book 3: Death on the Quai
Book 4: Death in Montmartre
Book 5: A Little Paris Christmas Murder - a novella
Book 6: Death at the Eiffel Tower

Evan also writes the *Isa Floris* thrillers that blend together far-flung
locations, ancient secrets and fast-paced action in an intriguing mix
of fact and fiction aimed at keeping you on the edge of your seat.

Books in the series are stand-alones and can be read in any order.

Book 1: The Aquarius Prophecy
Book 2: The Paradise Betrayal

CHAPTER 1

It was the best of times, it was the worst of times, and it was only Thursday...

Curled up in bed, Ava Sext watched the rain bounce off her apartment's glass roof. The raindrops fell in a repetitive manner and made a hypnotic pinging sound as they hit the glass. It was a summer rain -- a rain that was welcome after the long string of stiflingly hot days that Paris had been experiencing.

The weather report had predicted rain only for late this afternoon. But what did the weather report know? It had started raining in the middle of the night and hadn't stopped since.

It didn't matter when the rain had started. The downpour meant that Ava, who sold used books from an outdoor stand overlooking the Seine River, had a reason to stay home and do nothing until it stopped.

Listening to the sound of the raindrops cheered her. By the

time she got to her stand, the air would be crisp and clean. The leaves on the trees on the quay below would appear greener. The cobblestones along the river would glisten in the sunlight. The Seine River would flow by, revitalized by this manna from heaven.

Summer rain was a gift. It was not something to complain about.

Not wanting to waste an instant, Ava pulled her long frame out of bed and stretched her arms high in the air as she slipped her feet into her bluebird blue Moroccan slippers.

Striding across the loft apartment that had once been a series of maids' rooms, she slowed in front of the record player to choose an album from her late uncle's collection of 60s and 70's rock. After hesitating between Judy Collins and Steppenwolf, she chose the latter. What she needed was music to jog her awake.

She carefully placed the needle on her favorite song. As the first notes of "Born to be Wild" rang through the apartment, she headed to the kitchen with new spring in her step.

Almost dancing, she took a package of special ground Italian coffee off a shelf and measured it out. She put it in an espresso maker, added water and turned on the gas burner.

Looking down, she noticed that Mercury's bowl was still full. He had decided to skip breakfast. Ava didn't know what the cat's name was. She called him Mercury because, like the planet, he appeared most mornings. He'd slip into the apartment through an open window and head straight to the kitchen. Mercury was black with slanted green eyes. He was well fed and well groomed. For some reason, he had decided that it was her job to give him breakfast. For all she knew, her place just might be one stop on his breakfast tour of the neighborhood.

Ava had learned one thing from their brief relationship -- Mercury was a fair-weather cat. He didn't appear on rainy days, snowy days (not that there were many of them in Paris) or on windy days.

As the strong aroma of brewing coffee filled the kitchen, Ava inhaled deeply. She poured some coffee into her favorite mug: the one with the Union Jack Flag on it. For the briefest of moments, a ripple of homesickness ran through her.

Ava was a transplanted Londoner who had lived in Paris for less than a year.

She owed her presence in the city to her late Uncle Charles. After receiving a large inheritance, Charles Sext, a New Scotland Yard detective, had quit the force and moved to France to run an outdoor bookstand in Paris, having decided to enjoy life far from crime and criminals with a glass of good Bordeaux and as many books as he could read.

When Charles died, he left Ava his apartment in Paris and a monthly stipend on the condition that she lived there for a year.

More than money, her uncle had left her a philosophy:

Take time to live life.

For Ava, good coffee was an important part of living life. It was also the first step to a perfect day.

Sitting at the large wooden table that separated the kitchen from the rest of the apartment, she sipped her coffee slowly, savoring its earthy flavor.

Reflecting on her time in Paris, she liked to think that she had become a little bit Parisian. For one thing, she complained about the weather. London's weather was far worse than Paris's weather, but Londoners didn't complain about it. They took it in stride. If a tornado swept through Trafalgar Square, Ava was sure that many London residents would ignore it and go about their day.

In Paris, complaining about the weather was standard conversational fare. Rain or shine, it was the one subject that Parisians always circled back to. Ava suspected that it had very little to do with the weather and a lot to do with the complainer's outlook on life.

Just yesterday, Ava had bought a crispy *baguette* for dinner at her local *boulangerie*. When she had commented on the beautiful weather, the woman selling bread had frowned and had shaken her head ominously.

"It's nice today, but tomorrow who knows?" the woman said, arching her eyebrows as if a tsunami was about to hit Paris.

For some inexplicable reason, Ava had an urge to complain about today's rain. It was like an itch she couldn't scratch. She wondered what it meant. Checking the time, she saw that it was too late to call Benji in New York. Benji was a doctoral student in medieval manuscripts. They had had a brief whirlwind romance. It wasn't a romance that made fireworks go off. It was what the French call "*une amitié amoureuse*", a romantic friendship. Whatever you called it, Benji had done wonders for her morale. But he was in New York, she was in Paris, and neither of them had any desire to change that.

Last week, when Benji had suggested that it was time to move on, Ava hadn't disagreed with him. As long as she could keep the friendship part of their romantic friendship, she was fine.

Restless, she stood up and poured herself more coffee, taking care to leave some for later.

Sipping it, she frowned. It wasn't the rain or the end of her relationship with Benji that was bothering her. It was something more deep-seated.

She paced over to the record player, picked the needle up and put it on the track "Born to be Wild". Listening to the lyrics, a feverish agitation bubbled up inside her.

What she needed was excitement.

She needed something *inattendu* to happen... something totally unexpected.

In London, she would have said she was bored. But this was Paris, home of Sartre and Simone de Beauvoir, philosophers who had sipped cocktails at *Les Deux Magots* café while chain-smoking and speaking about existentialism: the confusion of the individual when faced with the meaninglessness of the modern world.

What Ava was experiencing was an existential crisis.

Why was she alive?

What was she going to do with her life?

Did life even have meaning?

Ava needed the heavens to open and shoot lightning bolts from the sky to shake her from this crisis of nothingness that she had fallen into.

What she needed for lack of a better term was a "somethingness".

When she had accepted the conditions in her late uncle's will, what had tipped the balance was having time to figure out what she wanted to do with her life.

Ava didn't regret for an instant leaving her London job in a boutique PR firm where her days and nights had been devoted to posting social media posts for celebrity clients.

She loved selling books. She loved Paris. But most of all,

she loved sleuthing -- a talent she shared with her late uncle.

Ava had only worked on a few cases, but she had quickly discovered that sleuthing was exciting, intellectually stimulating and adrenaline-packed.

It was also highly addictive.

Perhaps, what lay at the heart of her existential crisis was that she was a crime-junkie waiting for a crime to happen.

It didn't have to be murder.

It could be fraud, blackmail, or even petty theft.

Instead, it was raining.

If someone asked her about the rain in her present state of mind, she would tell them that after the rain came the sun.

And that was what she needed... a sunny adventure to light up her life.

Looking up, Ava saw that the rain had stopped.

It was time to get dressed.

She finished her coffee and put the cup in the sink. Then, she walked to the record player and moved the needle back to listen to "Born to be Wild" one last time for inspiration.

Suddenly, a ray of dazzling sunshine burst through the

glass roof and lit up the apartment. If this were a film instead of a book, Ava would have heard the earth shake and the heavens roar. She might even have heard the trumpeting of angels' horns.

Instead, she heard her doorbell ring.

Or didn't.

As she crossed the apartment, she heard a strange knocking sound. Turning, she eyed the pipes in the kitchen. They had a habit of knocking when the next-door neighbor ran his washing machine.

It took her a few seconds to realize that the knocking wasn't coming from the pipes. It was coming from her front door.

"I'm on my way," Ava shouted as she turned the music off. The sound of knocking and the tinny ringing sound of her doorbell now echoed through the apartment. After a quick inspection of what she was wearing -- flowered pajama bottoms and a rock concert T-shirt -- she headed to the door.

Turning the key twice in the lock, she unlocked the door and swung it open.

A tiny woman, soaked from head to foot, was standing on Ava's doormat. The woman had a pen in one hand and a business card in the other. Two cameras were slung across her chest.

Seeing Ava, the woman pushed her curly damp hair behind her ear, smiled and waved the business card in the air. "I was just writing you a note. I'm so lucky that you answered the door!"

Lucky!

A shiver of anticipation ran through Ava.

This was a sign.

Hearing a loud meowing behind her, Ava turned. Mercury was standing there staring at the woman with suspicion.

When it rains, it pours...

CHAPTER 2

Dismayed, the soaked woman standing in Ava's doorway eyed the puddle that was forming around her feet. She looked up and sighed. "Sorry about the deluge. My umbrella blew away when I was on the roof next door. I tried to catch it, but it was gone in a flash. Can I come in?"

"Of course," Ava said, swinging the door wide open.

Before entering, the woman bent over and removed her wet shoes. She winced when she saw a hole in one of her socks. "A wardrobe malfunction, and it's not even lunchtime."

Recognizing a kindred spirit, Ava grinned. "I have some cold coffee left from breakfast if you'd like some."

"Sold!" the woman said without the slightest hesitation. She followed Ava to the kitchen where Ava poured the remaining coffee into a mug.

The woman took the mug and cradled it in both hands. "Introductions are in order. I'm Loulou Pleyel, a location scout for a film production company. I was taking photos on a neighboring roof when I saw your tower. I knew we had to have it."

Ava was puzzled. "For what?"

"Our film," Loulou replied. She pointed at the tower. "I've never seen anything like it in Paris. It's unique."

Ava glanced up at it and smiled. "It's my favorite spot on starry evenings. I can sit there for hours watching the sky."

"I warn you. I'm persistent. If I don't get your tower, I'll pester you until I do!" Loulou said as she downed her coffee.

Ava laughed. There was something wonderfully warm about Loulou and incredibly exciting at the same time. Ava couldn't shake the notion that Loulou Pleyel was a sign from the heavens that something was about to happen, something momentous.

Loulou handed Ava her business card.

An amused look spread across Ava's face as she read it. "Catastrophe Productions? Is that really a good name for a film company?"

"Have you ever worked in film?" Loulou asked.

"Once," Ava confessed as if admitting a crime. "I worked as a production assistant on a student film in London."

"How did that work out for you?"

"It was like riding a roller coaster blindfolded," Ava admitted. "I still have nightmares about it."

Loulou's eyes danced. "Films are one catastrophe after another. Making a film is like building a sandcastle during a category five hurricane. Anything and everything can throw the film off track and does. But somehow we muddle through, and the film gets made."

"The magic of cinema?" Ava suggested tongue-in-cheek.

"Exactly!" Loulou replied with a wicked grin. She stepped into the center of Ava's apartment and held up one of her cameras. "May I?"

"Please!" Ava said, delighted at the idea that her tower might be in a film.

Loulou began taking photos. "This is a wonderful apartment. It's like a film set. I can see a remake of the Audrey Hepburn film *Roman Holiday* taking place here."

"Do you often work with Catastrophe Productions?" Ava asked, curious to learn more about the energetic woman before her.

"This is the first time. Believe me, it's the last. We start shooting on Monday, and they're still rewriting the script and requesting location changes. I took over from a friend who had the bad luck to lose some of her photos. They disappeared from the main set. She quit, and I took over."

A ripple of anticipation ran up Ava's spine... *Burglary! Now they were getting somewhere.*

"Does she know who took them?" Ava asked.

"She said the set was haunted," Loulou replied.

Ava's eyes went round. "Haunted?"

"That was my reaction. Why would a ghost want her photos? In films, ghosts want revenge. Or they appear to solve a mystery. In my opinion, the production manager was behind it. He and my friend were dating. Maybe he took the photos so she'd quit. Or she took them so he'd fire her," Loulou said as she lay down on her back to take pictures of the glass ceiling. "Working with someone you date is not easy. The production manager is very efficient, but at times he's strange. Oops! I shouldn't have said that. You probably won't want us to use your tower now."

"On the contrary, I like strange people," Ava sputtered. "What's the film about?"

"The pitch? It's a suspense-filled heist film. A love story. It has almost everything in it. If the screenwriter doesn't stop making changes, it will have everything in it."

"That's why you were on the roof this morning?"

"In a rainstorm!" Loulou said as she rose to her feet. "They added a rooftop scene three days ago. I'm lucky it wasn't a scene on the bottom of the river, or I'd be out there now in a wetsuit. Can I see the tower?"

"Of course." Ava walked to the tower door and unlocked it. "I keep it locked because the door swings open if I don't. I've tried repairing it, but the door has a mind of its own."

"I once worked on an "aliens from another planet" genre film. The aliens were invisible. You wouldn't even notice they were there until…"

"The door banged?" Ava asked, raising her eyebrows.

"Or the floorboard creaked. How stupid is that? If I'd been the director, I would have added some smoke or an odd sound that only the hero could hear. But what do I know? I'm the location scout." Loulou said as she started up the stairs.

Feeling something brush against her leg, Ava looked down. Alarmed, Mercury was eyeing the tower door. Ava crouched down next to the cat.

"There's nothing to worry about. Loulou works in film. Everyone is like that. If you play your cards right, you might even get a close-up!"

Mercury's whiskers quivered. He turned and walked away.

"Suit yourself," Ava said to the departing animal.

"This is great!" Loulou shouted down from the tower. "Better than I'd imagined."

Ava stood up and dashed up the stairs.

Loulou pointed at the neighboring roof. "Imagine. A couple is standing there, hidden by the chimney pipes. It's a dark, moonless night. It's their last chance to carry off the robbery. They're tense."

Ava looked at the roof and raised an eyebrow. "Wouldn't that be a dangerous scene to shoot?"

Loulou shook her head. "No. They'll be wearing body harnesses."

"Why don't they shoot it in a studio?" Ava asked.

"It's too late to build the set now, and it would be too costly," Loulou replied.

"What happens next?" Ava asked, curious about the story.

"The couple creep silently across the roof."

Ava's eyes lit up. "Like Cary Grant in *To Catch A Thief*... Who are the actors?"

Loulou leaned out the window to take more photos. "Vincent

Rennel, Ludmila Tarakov and Ian Granger."

Recognizing the last name, Ava perked up. She had never heard of the other two, but Ian Granger had starred in a popular UK TV series. "The film is in English?"

"Yes. It's a French-English co-production." Loulou moved to another window, swung it open and hung out to take photos of Ava's apartment below. "Have you lived here long?"

"Almost a year," Ava said.

"You're lucky to have found this place. In my job, I've seen hundreds of apartments. Yours is exceptional, and the location is fabulous. You know what they say about real estate?"

Ava grinned. "Location, location, location."

"Absolutely. How did you find it?" Loulou asked.

"It belonged to my late uncle," Ava replied.

"With the tower, it's like you're a princess waiting to be rescued."

Ava burst out laughing. "More like a princess waiting to fight dragons! I'm a lot tougher than I look."

Loulou nodded approvingly. "Women have to be tough. Once we learn that, life is much easier." She pointed to the window. "Could you stand there?"

Ava hesitated, puzzled.

"It's to get some size perspective for the camera. I know the tower is perfect, but I need to convince the director and the production team."

Ava stepped over to the window. Loulou took several photos of her from different angles.

"In a way, I shouldn't complain about the production," Loulou said.

"Why?" Ava asked.

"In my last job, the former location scout on this project and I spent weeks underground looking at every cellar in Paris. We even crawled around the catacombs and sewer tunnels. It was for a big-budget American film. In the end, they shot the film in Prague." Loulou sighed. "I never want to see another cellar as long as I live. I'm happy to be running around rooftops."

"Even in the rain?" Ava asked.

"Even in the rain," Loulou confirmed. "Did you know that some of the cellars in this neighborhood used to connect? They formed an underground tunnel that ran down to the Seine."

Ava's eyes lit up. "Secret tunnels? That sounds exciting."

"Not if you're claustrophobic like I am," Loulou said as she pointed at the other window. "Could you stand there? I want one or two last shots before I go."

Ava moved to the window. "Do the tunnels still exist?"

Loulou shook her head. "Over the years, most were walled up. Some collapsed. And if some still exist, we didn't find them." She took one last photo and checked it in the camera's viewing screen. "Can I have your cell phone number?"

Ava took a piece of paper off the desk, jotted down her number and handed it to Loulou.

Loulou put the paper in her pocket. "If the production company is interested, what's the best time for them to come see the tower? They'll need to verify that it works from a technical standpoint."

"Anytime is good. I work right down the street on the Quai Malaquais. I'm a bookseller."

Loulou was astonished. "I've always wondered who sold books there."

"Now you know," Ava said with a warm smile.

Loulou and Ava walked down the steps to the apartment.

"I'm sure the production will like the tower. They'd be crazy not to. Besides, I'm not thrilled about continuing to wander over rooftops. It's already cost me one umbrella," Loulou said with a shudder.

The women walked to the door. Ava glanced at the kitchen. There was no sign of Mercury.

As she put on her shoes, Loulou took another look at Ava's apartment. "It's really magical. If for some reason the production company doesn't want it, I'll keep it in mind for other films."

Suddenly, the tower door swung open and banged noisily against the wall.

"Aliens!" Loulou and Ava said at the same time.

As soon as Loulou had left, Ava dashed across the apartment to the record player and put on "Born to be Wild". Somethingness had arrived, and she was ready!

CHAPTER 3

Ava waltzed down the rue des Saints-Pères toward the Seine River. Her existential crisis had vanished. Every bone in her body was shouting that something exciting was about to happen. Loulou Pleyel was the first sign of that. Now all Ava had to do was to wait for what was coming next.

When she reached Café Zola, "her café", she waved at Gerard who was setting up tables outside dressed in the traditional French waiter uniform of black trousers, a white shirt and a long black apron.

"Lovely day, Gerard!" Ava shouted out.

In response, Gerard narrowed his eyes and stared up at the cloudless sky. "Until it starts raining again!"

Ava continued on her way. Gerard's grumpiness was part of

his charm.

When the traffic light changed to green, she dashed across the Quai Malaquais and came to a halt in front of the 8.60 meters of bottle-green wooden boxes that were perched on a stone wall overlooking the river below.

This was Ava's personal fiefdom -- her kingdom.

Ava was a "*bouquinist*": a bookseller. Since 1859, concessions to the green boxes that ran from the Pont Marie to the Quai de Louvre on the right bank and from the Quai de la Tournelle to the Quai Voltaire on the left bank had been granted by the city of Paris to a lucky few.

Ava belonged to that select group.

She unlocked the padlocks on her boxes, flung their wooden tops open and breathed in deeply. The books inside had a special odor that was exhilarating. After a quick glance at the Louvre Museum across the way, Ava removed a green and white lawn chair from one of the boxes, carried it over to a tree and set it up in the shade. A few drops of water fell on her from the leaves overhead.

A gift from on high, Ava thought as she ran her tongue over a drop that had fallen on her top lip.

"Morning, Ava", a familiar voice said.

Looking up, Ava saw her neighboring bookseller, Ali Beltran, walking toward her. A trim man in his thirties, Ali was a graduate of the well-known Paris art school, the *Beaux Arts* Academy. When he wasn't painting, he ran the bookstand with his twin brother, Hassan.

Ali pushed the heavy horn-rimmed glasses that gave him a gravitas that hid a wicked sense of humor up his nose and stared at her, puzzled. "I didn't expect to see you this early on a rainy day."

Ava feigned indignation. "I'm not some frail flower that wilts at the first raindrop."

Unsure of whether she was joking or not, Ali shook his head. "No one would ever say that about you, Ava. Ever."

"Thank you," Ava replied and burst out laughing.

Ali studied her with raised eyebrows. "Something is different about you. Have you won the lottery or written a best-selling novel?"

"Both," Ava replied.

Always interested in gossip, Ali's eyes lit up. "Tell me."

"This morning, I was in the throes of an existential crisis. You know what I'm talking about?"

Ali reared back. "Of course, I'm French."

"I was in my apartment listening to the rain beat down, while reflecting on nothingness and somethingness, and then it happened," Ava said as dramatically as possible.

Not taking the bait, Ali waited patiently for her to finish.

"Someone knocked on my door!" Ava announced.

"A lover with a winning lottery ticket?"

"Even better! It was a location scout. She wants to use my tower in a film. Isn't that magical?"

"What type of film?" Ali asked with real interest.

"It's a bit of everything... a heist film with love, action and suspense. There are also cat burglars who run across rooftops. That's all I know." Ava handed him Loulou's card. "Have you ever heard of the production company?"

Ali read the card and raised an eyebrow. "Catastrophe Productions? From what I know that describes film production to a T."

Ava was astonished. "You worked in film?"

Ali nodded. "When I was a student at art school, I painted film sets for a vampire film set in Paris. They reconstructed the city in a studio. I wonder if they're going to reconstruct your tower in a studio?"

"Loulou said they don't have the time or the budget. I'd be disappointed if they did. I want them to film in my tower. I wish Uncle Charles were alive. He'd think it was wonderful."

"It's a sign of something," Ali said with a knowing look. "You were going through an existential crisis, and then there was the fatal knock on the door…"

"Fatal?" Ava asked, startled.

"Fatal in the sense that it changed the status quo. Now you have to wait for the next action that will inevitably occur. Synchronicity!"

Synchronicity was Ali's favorite theory. Synchronicity posited that two seemingly unrelated events were often cosmically linked.

Content that Ali thought that a significant event was about to occur, Ava eyed a stand further down the quay that was still shuttered. "Have you spoken with Henri today?"

"He'll be here for lunch at Café Zola," Ali announced.

Henri DeAth was a fellow bookseller. He was also a former French *notaire*, a notary. In France, notaries belonged to a powerful caste. They were wealthy, secretive and protective of their privileges, which went back hundreds of years.

Henri often joked, "Not only do we know where the bodies are buried, we helped bury them…"

Yet Henri had given it all up to become a bookseller on the Seine. A French notary giving up his practice before he was in his dotage or dead was as rare as Christmas in August…

Impossible.

However, for Henri nothing was impossible.

At a mere sixty, he had sold his practice to his nephew and moved to Paris. Henri had been Charles Sext's best friend and his partner in sleuthing. Henri had become Ava's partner in sleuthing since they had saved Yves Dubois, a university professor, from being murdered.

Henri was also the most accomplished and surprising person that Ava had ever met. He was constantly astounding her with his wealth of knowledge. Her uncle might be dead, but Henri was alive and well.

"Did Henri say what the café is serving for lunch?" Ava asked.

Ali knitted his brows together, trying to remember. "Sea bream carpaccio."

Ava's eyes lit up. "With bergamot and coriander?"

"Would Alain do it any other way?" Ali asked with a smile.

Alain was the chef at Café Zola. He ran the café with his cousin, the ill-tempered, yet otherwise charming, Gerard.

At the thought of sea bream, Ava's mouth watered. Sea bream carpaccio would go perfectly with a light white wine. Perhaps a Chenin Blanc or a Chablis.

"Did he tell you what was for dessert?" Ava asked.

"Poached pears with homemade vanilla ice cream," Ali

replied. "I've already reserved one."

"How am I going to make it to lunch?" Ava asked, checking the time.

"You'll survive. I have some iced coffee if you'd like," Ali said.

Ava grinned. "That would be great." Ali's iced coffee was sensational. His most recent brew had cardamom and mint thrown in. It was odd but delicious.

Ali strode off to his stand. Seconds later, he returned with a cooler cup in one hand and a thick book in the other. "It's a survey of world cinema. It has good sections on French and British film."

"Thanks." Ava took the cup and the book and settled into her chair. Her day was getting better and better. First Loulou Pleyel, then sea bream carpaccio and now delicious iced coffee and a book to read... *What next?*

Knowing that the next was inevitably coming made the morning fly by.

Customers stopped by Ava's stand and purchased books as if it there was a fire sale going on. She sold an entire series of guide books to Italy from the 1970s, three French thrillers, a comic book and a DVD on sharks. She also sold four Mona Lisa mugs and a gravy bowl.

Between sales, Ava plunged into French film history. She was astonished to learn that Jean Renoir, the famous French director was the son of Renoir, the painter. A lot of the French shared the same last names. The head of security at the Louvre who had helped Ava in a recent case was called Claude Monet. Despite having the same name, he was not related to the painter. However, as Ava's Claude Monet worked at the Louvre, you could say there was a special link between the two men.

"Are you ready for your close-up?" a deep male voice asked.

Startled, Ava looked up from her book. Immediately, a wide grin spread across her face. She jumped up and hugged the tall well-built man with dark hair in his early thirties who was standing in front of her. "Jaspar! What are you doing in Paris? How did you find me?"

Jaspar held out his phone. There was a photo of Ava at her tower window on the screen.

"You know Loulou Pleyel?"

Jaspar nodded. "She works for my production company."

"Catastrophe Productions?" Ava asked, incredulous.

"That's my coproducer, the French production company. My company is Silver Print Productions." Jaspar looked at her clothing and blinked. "I'm having a *déjà vu* experience. Weren't you wearing that same jacket the last time I saw you?"

Ava looked down at the khaki safari jacket she was wearing. It had a very recognizable leaping tiger embroidered on its sleeve.

"After Loulou came by, I dug it out of the closet in memory of my short-lived film career. How is your father?"

Jaspar's father, Graham Porter, was a well-known investigative journalist who worked all over the world.

Jaspar shrugged. "Last I heard he was in Asia. I sent him an email telling him that I was shooting in Paris. He once lived here and loves the city. I was hoping he'd come for the shoot. Instead, he emailed me back to say he was busy."

Too late, Ava remembered that Jaspar rarely saw his father. He once said that if he wanted to see him, he'd turn on the BBC.

"How is your Uncle Charles?" Jaspar asked.

Jaspar and Ava's uncle had bonded from the moment they met.

"He died a year ago," Ava replied.

Jaspar put his hand on Ava's shoulder. "I'm sorry to hear that."

A shiver ran through Ava as he touched her. "It wasn't unexpected. Uncle Charles wouldn't want us to be sad. On the contrary..."

"I was hoping to talk with him. I have a problem I need advice on," Jaspar said with a sigh.

Ava stood up taller. "A Scotland Yard type problem?"

Uneasy, Jaspar shifted from foot to foot. "I'm not sure. I was hoping your uncle could tell me. As soon as I saw your photo, I called Loulou. She told me where to find you. Is there someplace we could have a sandwich and coffee? I'm starved."

"A sandwich? In Paris? Don't be ridiculous." Ava checked the time. It was lunchtime at Café Zola. She walked over to Ali who was hovering nearby. "Ali, this is Jaspar Porter. I helped him on his student film in London years ago. Guess what? He's involved with my film!"

"Catastrophe Productions?" Ali asked with shining eyes.

Jaspar nodded. "That's my French coproducer."

"Synchronicity! What did I tell you?" Ali said to Ava, ecstatic that he had been right.

"Can you watch my stand while we eat?" Ava asked.

"Of course!" Ali eyed Jaspar with a mysterious smile. "You're in for a life-changing experience."

Jaspar looked worried.

CHAPTER 4

At Café Zola, Jaspar and Ava squeezed through the lunch crowd that was by now spilling out onto the sidewalk. It was the usual mix of locals, tourists, antique dealers and salespeople from the nearby luxury shops, along with a bookseller or two. Ava frayed her way toward the back of the café followed by Jaspar.

Visibly enchanted by the café's traditional decor: a zinc counter, old-fashioned wooden tables, immense gold-framed mirrors, red leather seats and brass fittings that shone in the sunlight, Jaspar slowed. "This is charming. It's like a film set for a Parisian café."

"It is a Parisian café," Ava said in a teasing tone. She had always gotten on well with Jaspar. From the short time they had spent together, she sensed that that had not changed.

At the back of the café, a handsome man in his sixties with deep blue eyes and salt and pepper hair that curled around his face was reading a book at a white-clothed table set for four.

When Ava reached the table, she smiled broadly. "Henri, I've brought a friend from London for lunch."

Always the gentleman, Henri rose to his feet. "I'm Henri DeAth."

"Jaspar Porter," Jaspar said as did a double-take looking at Henri. "Did anyone ever tell you that you look exactly like Ian Granger?"

"People have mentioned it once or twice. Although I think I'm better looking," Henri joked.

Jaspar slid into the red leather bench against the wall. "DeAth is an unusual last name…"

"It's Flemish," Ava explained. "*De* means from, and *Ath* is a city in Belgium. And yes, you heard right. Henri's last name is pronounced like the English word "death". That startles many people."

Henri gave Jaspar a lopsided grin. "It's led to some odd looks over the years. Are you here on a visit?"

Jaspar shook his head. "I'm here for work. I'm making a film… Or at least trying to."

Ava's face lit up when she heard the word "film". "This morning, I was in the middle of an existential crisis when a location scout showed up at my apartment to take pictures of my tower. She sent them to Jaspar, and here he is."

"And the crisis?" Henri asked.

Ava snapped her fingers. "Gone. Just like that."

Jaspar held up his phone and showed Henri the photos. "I couldn't believe it when I received the photos. I hadn't seen Ava in years, and there she was on my screen."

Henri looked from Ava to Jaspar. "How did you two meet?"

Jaspar turned toward Ava. "We worked together on a student film I directed years ago."

"Briefly. I believe you fired me," Ava said, amused.

"You quit," Jaspar protested.

Ava shook her head. "I tried to quit. You told me that volunteers couldn't quit, they could only be fired."

Henri attempted to hide his smile. "What happened then?"

"I was back on the set the next day," Ava admitted.

"Free production assistants are hard to find. Free production assistants who are efficient are even rarer," Jaspar added with a knowing nod.

"And the film?" Henri asked Jaspar. "Did it bring you fame and glory?"

Jaspar snorted. "No. It won a few prizes. The experience convinced me that I was not cut out to be a director. I moved into film production, and I'm still there."

"That's a tough business," Henri said.

"It is. But you're never bored," Jaspar countered.

Ava smiled. "His company is producing a film here in Paris. His coproducer's company is called Catastrophe Productions!"

Henri burst out laughing. "I hope that's not premonitory."

"That was my reaction when I heard the name. However, necessity is the mother of invention," Jaspar said in a tone of voice that let on that there was more that he wasn't saying.

Gerard walked up to their table. Brimming with energy, he took a pencil from behind his ear and flipped over the page of a tiny notepad. "Sea bream carpaccio for everyone?"

Jaspar shook his head. "I'll just have a sandwich."

"Alain would be upset if you ordered a sandwich," Gerard replied, arching his eyebrows.

Ava turned to Jaspar. "Alain is the chef. The first time I came here, I ordered a sandwich. Alain was so outraged he came out of the kitchen to change my mind. I can still remember what he served me. *Coq au vin*, rooster in wine sauce, and a *tarte tatin*, a caramelized upside-down apple tart, for dessert. I've never looked back," Ava said with a wistful smile.

"You wouldn't want Alain to come out of the kitchen and wrestle you down," Henri joked to Jaspar.

"As a film producer, I've learned that self-preservation is all," Jaspar replied. He eyed Gerard. "I'm in for the carpaccio."

Gerard nodded. "With a light white wine." He turned and left without waiting for an answer.

"How did you choose Catastrophe Productions as a coproducer?" Henri asked.

"The person financing the film chose it. I suppose he had his reasons," Jaspar replied.

Gerard reappeared with a bottle of white wine. "It's a Muscadet from the Loire Valley in France," he announced as he uncorked it and poured some in Henri's glass.

Henri took a sip and gave a short nod of approval. "Sheer perfection as always."

Content, Gerard poured wine in everyone's glasses.

Ava raised her glass in the air. "To catastrophes!"

Jaspar hesitated.

"To avoiding catastrophes," Henri suggested.

"That I can drink to…" Jaspar said with visible relief.

As the chilled white wine with touches of citrus hit her palate, Ava was in heaven. Still, business was business. She put her glass down and leaned toward Henri. "Jaspar told me odd things are going on with the film."

"Odd is an understatement! The film was cursed from the beginning, and it's gotten worse each day," Jaspar said with a sigh.

"Loulou told me that the first location scout had some of her photos stolen," Ava said.

Jaspar pursed his lips. "I wouldn't say stolen. That would be jumping to conclusions. She lost some photos of rooftops from our film and some photos from her last film."

"From the big American production that had her crawling around every cellar, catacomb and underground tunnel in Paris?" Ava asked.

"The very same. Her backup on the cloud also vanished. It was probably human error or a virus. She might even have deleted them herself by accident," Jaspar explained. "We work long hours. Mistakes get made."

"Why do you say the film was cursed from the beginning?"

Henri asked as he sipped his wine.

"Usually it's the financing that trips you up in film. Getting the money can take an eternity. One of my films took over five years to finance."

"Five years!" Henri said, astonished.

Jaspar nodded. "You go from film board to film board to apply for funding. You need contracts with TV stations. Actors have to commit to a film that might not even get made. Along the way, you lose an actor or a TV station and have to start over again. This time, funding was a piece of cake. A wealthy writer wanted his book to be made into a film at any cost. The last part is what drew me in."

"That doesn't sound so complicated," Henri said.

"That's what I thought," Jaspar replied as he took a piece of crispy bread from the breadbasket. "However, I never met the writer financing the film. We work through his lawyer. And the writer had a lot of contractual demands."

"What's the writer's name," Ava asked.

"Alan Smith, a pen name. I have no idea who Alan Smith is. Obviously he has money, or he wouldn't be financing a film."

"What sort of demands did he make?" Henri asked.

Ava eyed Henri. His voice had taken on his sleuthing tone, a tone that meant he would leave no stone unturned to discover what was going on.

"First, he imposed a screenwriter on us who is cantankerous. I'd add unpleasant and volatile, but I wouldn't want to impugn his character," Jaspar said in a tone, which implied that was exactly what he wanted to do.

Listening intently to what Jaspar was saying, Henri took another sip of wine. "What's the film about?"

"It's a robbery. A jewel is stolen. The jewel disappears. A barge on the Seine blows up. The suspects vanish. We never learn what happened to the jewel or the suspects."

"Is that the recipe for a successful film?" Henri asked.

Jaspar burst out laughing. "No. In a heist film, people want to know what happened. The writer did say we could rework the end. That's what the screenwriter has been doing for weeks, and we still don't have it."

Gerard arrived with their food. He set the sea bream carpaccio on the table. Ava could feel her mouth water. It looked delicious.

Gerard took out his notepad. "Three pear desserts?"

"There's more?" Jaspar asked as he eyed the feast in front of him.

"You're in France," Gerard replied with a whiff of reproach.

"Enough of your gastronomic proselytizing, Gerard. Let him eat his meal. But yes, put three pear desserts aside," Henri said.

Ava turned to Jaspar. "They're served with homemade vanilla ice cream."

Both Henri and Ava watched Jaspar take his first bite of carpaccio.

As Jaspar chewed and swallowed, his face lit up. "It's fabulous! I understand why Ali said I was in for a life-changing experience."

"Now you know where to come," Henri said. "My table is always reserved. You're welcome to join me any time."

Jaspar beamed. "I'll take you up on that."

A thought struck Ava. "You still don't have the end? Doesn't shooting start next week?"

"Yes. But as you know, a film isn't shot in order," Jaspar said with a frown. "I warned Martin... Martin Scotsdale, the screenwriter, that if he didn't have the end by this Saturday, I'd have the director rewrite it."

"Can you do that under your contract?" Ava asked.

"No. But Martin doesn't know the terms of our contract. He truly believes that he was chosen because of his talent," Jaspar said with a deep sigh. "Just like Simon Heppleworth, the director."

"What is Heppleworth like?" Henri asked.

Jaspar took a sip of wine. "Uninvolved. He's in it for the money and doesn't hide it. He's been in Paris for three weeks and is totally content to let the production run with everything. He just checks in when he feels like it and does the bare minimum."

"Couldn't the director and screenwriter write the end together?" Ava asked.

"I wish they would. They haven't even met. Given their personalities, I expect fireworks when they do meet."

"Why did you accept to produce the film under these conditions?" Henri asked.

"Money. My production company was about to close. I owed back taxes. This film will save me. There's even a hefty production bonus for the producers if it gets made," Jaspar explained.

Frowning, Henri sat back in his seat. "Is that unusual?"

"Very unusual. I wasn't in a position to look a gift horse in the mouth," Jaspar said.

"And now?" Henri asked.

"It's too late. We have an expression in the UK "*in for a penny, in for a pound*". That's my situation."

"Tell me about Catastrophe Productions," Henri said as he took a bite of carpaccio.

"Catastrophe Productions was also desperate. The owner is a nice guy but clueless. He's never made a feature film. In fact, he's only made two short films. As anyone can tell you, films don't scale. The problems you encounter on a short film are much different than those you encounter on a feature film. Lance LeGris is well-meaning, but he's young. He's only 25. He doesn't see the problems barreling down at us. He keeps saying it will all work out in the end."

"That implies that there is an end," Henri said.

Jaspar looked alarmed.

"What's the title of the film?" Ava asked.

"*Death on the Quai*," Jaspar replied as he took a long sip of wine. "I should have taken that as a sign."

"Of what?" Ava asked, worried.

"Of my imminent demise. The production office is a block from the quay. If things don't change, the stress will kill me."

"Where are you filming on Monday?" Ava asked.

"We shoot an explosion on a barge Monday and Tuesday. We'll be shooting at night. It's complicated because we're using explosives. So far, we've got the river patrol, the prefecture of police, the city of Paris, the fire department and explosion specialists involved... Not to mention the insurance companies."

"You're going to blow up a barge?" Henri asked as he poured everyone more wine.

Jaspar shook his head. "We don't have the budget for that. It will be all smoke and mirrors. Nate, the production manager, assures me that it will look real. I believe him."

Ava frowned. Nate must be the man that the former location scout was dating when she quit.

Henri sipped his wine. "Where is your production office?"

"Just down the street. We're near *La Monnaie*, the French Mint," Jaspar replied.

"That an upscale neighborhood for a small production company," Henri said.

Jaspar nodded. "It is. Lance's aunt, Madame LeGris, owns the building. It's a hôtel particulier -- a mansion. She's given us the former coach house. It's a fabulous space. We're lucky to have it."

Henri was now truly astonished. "Lance is from the LeGris Jewelers family?"

Jaspar shrugged. "I guess so. He did mention that his late uncle was a jeweler."

"Louis LeGris was more than a jeweler. He was a jeweler who sold ridiculously expensive baubles to the international jet set throughout the 70s and 80s. Then he moved to Switzerland and lived on a mountain top," Henri said in clear admiration.

"When you're that rich, I suppose you can do anything," Jaspar replied.

"Could someone be trying to sabotage the production?" Ava asked as her mind went back to the missing photos.

Jaspar knitted his eyebrows together. "That occurred to me. But why? The way things are going the film will blow up on its own."

"Loulou said that the production manager might have taken the missing photos," Ava said as she turned to Henri. "He and the former location scout were seeing each other."

Jaspar shook his head. "I don't believe that for an instant. Nate loves women, but he's a pro. He would never do anything to hurt the production. The former location scout might have gotten rid of the photos herself."

Ava was puzzled. "Why?"

"Nate had moved on. There's nothing unusual about that. Films shoots are a hotbed of short-lived romance."

"Whatever happened to Sally?" Ava blurted out before she could stop herself.

Jaspar was taken aback. "Sally... Sally Jenkins? I haven't thought of her in years. Our fling during the shoot convinced me that film and love were not compatible."

"Do you still believe that?" Henri asked with a smile.

"I'm a confirmed bachelor," Jaspar replied, tightening his jaw.

Henri laughed. "At your age, I'd give it time."

Ava was happy to hear that Jaspar had forgotten Sally Jenkins. She had never liked her. During the shoot, Sally had spent the vast majority of her time batting her big blue eyes at Jaspar.

Gerard appeared. He removed their plates and set the pear desserts down in front of them.

Jaspar's eyes lit up. "The café needs an Instagram food page… This is beautiful!"

"It tastes even better," Ava replied as she took a spoonful.

"Tell me about you, Henri? You must be bored to tears hearing about film," Jaspar said.

"I'm a bookseller. Originally from Bordeaux. I was a good friend of Ava's late uncle.

Ava shook her head. "Henri's too modest. He's a former notary, an expert on almost everything, and he knows half the population of France. On any given day, you'll see people stream to his stand to talk with him."

"Aren't notaries some sort of secret group that controls the country?" Jaspar asked.

Henri laughed. "They wish. Booksellers probably know more secrets."

Ava doubted that anyone knew more secrets than Henri, not that he would ever reveal them.

"Henri worked on some cases with Uncle Charles," Ava said.

A look of relief ran across Jaspar's face. "Then maybe you can help me."

"Ava's done some sleuthing too since she's been in Paris," Henri added.

Jaspar smiled at Ava. "I'm not surprised. Ava was always fearless."

Ava took a spoon of ice cream. Loulou's visit had set off a cascade of events. But, so far, seeing Jaspar was the best of all.

"I have an idea!" Jaspar announced as he banged his hand on the table.

Startled, Henri and Ava stared at him.

"As the film's being shot in English, my assistant was coming from London this weekend to work on it. Why don't you take her place?"

"Won't your assistant be upset?" Ava asked.

"Absolutely not. She hates the director, loathes the screenwriter and wasn't happy about leaving her cat."

"I'd love to do it," Ava replied before Jaspar could change his mind.

Jaspar raised his glass. "A toast. To my new sleuthing partners."

Ava and Henri raised their glasses in the air.

Jaspar eyed Ava. "Now you have two jobs to do... production assistant and sleuth. But by being there *in situ*... How do you say that in French?"

"*Sur place*," Ava replied.

"By being *sur place*, you'll have a window into what's going on."

Suddenly, Jaspar's cell phone vibrated. He looked at the number. "It's Nate, the production manager." He answered the phone. As he listened, his features tightened, and his breathing became troubled. "OK. I'll be right there." He hung up and was silent.

"What is it?" Henri asked, worried.

Jaspar shook his head. "I don't know. Nate wouldn't tell me. All he said was that something's happened down on the quay." He turned to Ava. "Can you start your new job now?"

CHAPTER 5

Traffic on the Quai Malaquais was completely blocked. Cars were bumper to bumper. The honking was deafening. Frowning, Jaspar eyed the mass of vehicles as he and Ava stepped out of Café Zola.

"Should I call a taxi?" Ava asked, taking her phone out of her pocket.

Jaspar shook his head. "It will be faster by motorcycle. The production rented one for me. It's parked on the rue de Seine."

Ava started walking. The rue de Seine was one street over. They could be there in minutes. She was more excited than she wanted to admit about working on a film. She was especially content that she would be working with Jaspar.

Jaspar's cell phone rang. He eyed caller ID. "I have to answer this."

As they continued to walk, Ava studied Jaspar as he spoke on the phone. Things always went wrong in a film shoot. Why did he believe something odd was taking place? She wondered if he might be overreacting? However, her memory of him was that he was very level-headed and not at all prone to flights of fancy.

"Don't worry. I'm on my way," Jaspar said in a near whisper as he ended the call.

Ava slowed and eyed him. "Is it serious?" For the first time, she began to believe that Jaspar was right and that something was wrong.

Jaspar's face was wracked with worry. "Nate, the production manager, is a professional. Nothing fazes him, absolutely nothing. He's as tough as they come. Yet, he sounded spooked when I spoke to him earlier. That was Claire, the assistant director. She's no pushover, and she sounded spooked, too. She was so upset she could barely speak."

"Spooked? What do you mean?" Ava asked, surprised by Jaspar's choice of words.

Jaspar tightened his jaw. "It's as if something completely unnerved them, something they never expected to happen. In film, you learn to expect anything and everything. When I asked Claire to tell me what was going on, she repeated that they needed me at the set right away."

Ava tried to imagine what could be so terrible that they didn't want to tell Jaspar. The answers that came to her were disturbing.

"Is your coproducer joining us?" Ava asked as they continued walking.

Jaspar looked alarmed. "Lance? I hope not. Don't get me wrong. Lance is a nice guy, but he's a disaster on wheels. If he can make a situation worse, he will. He doesn't do it deliberately. It's in his DNA."

Reaching the rue de Seine, Jaspar strode up to a heavy touring motorcycle that was parked on the corner of the street. He unlocked its chain. "Paris traffic took some getting used to. With this monster, it's a dream." He opened the luggage trunk and took out a helmet and handed it to Ava. "

Despite the seriousness of the situation, Ava grinned when she saw the helmet's red devil horns.

"It came with the rental," Jaspar said with a sheepish grin. He placed the chain in the trunk, pulled a black helmet out and put it on.

"Where is the set?" Ava asked.

"The Quai Henri IV," Jaspar said as he pushed the motorcycle into the street.

Ava nodded. The Quai Henri IV was in the 4th arrondissement. It was across the river from the Arab World Institute. On a motorcycle, they could be there in fifteen minutes.

"Why did you decide to begin with the explosion? Even if it's only smoke and mirrors, it's a difficult scene to start with."

"We didn't have a choice. It's one of the only scenes Ian Granger isn't in. Ian's in Brazil finishing up a film. He can only join us at the end of next week."

"What do you think is wrong?" Ava asked.

"I'm praying it's a technical problem. The company carrying out the explosion was supposed to meet with the fire department and the river police this afternoon to go over the final details."

Ava tried to lighten the atmosphere. "Remember what you said when we worked together?"

"That was ages ago!" Jaspar protested.

Ava smiled. "It was my first shoot. It left an impression on me. You said that when things go wrong, it was better that they went wrong at the beginning."

Jaspar laughed. "If I remember correctly, during that shoot things went wrong at the beginning, in the middle and at the end. It was a running disaster... except for your participation."

More content with his remark than she'd like to admit, Ava climbed onto the touring seat.

Jaspar got on the bike and looked at Ava. "Ready?"

"Ready," she said as she pulled down her helmet's visor.

She leaned back against the luggage trunk as Jaspar drove down the rue de Seine. He turned onto the blocked Quai Malaquais and zigzagged around the stopped cars until he reached the bridge. Then, he turned right and drove over the bridge toward the Louvre. Turning right once again, he sped down the upper quay.

Despite the tense situation, Ava enjoyed the ride. The wind blowing over her was glorious, and she had an incredible view of some of Paris's most beautiful sites… the Louvre, the Conciergerie and the spires of Notre Dame.

Fifteen minutes later, they reached the Quai Henri IV. Jaspar slowed, pulled over and stopped at the top of a sloping access ramp. He parked the motorcycle behind three white vans.

"They belong to the production," Jaspar explained.

Ava hopped off the bike. She took her helmet off and handed it to Jaspar. He unlocked the luggage trunk and put the helmets inside. After relocking it, they walked down the ramp to the lower quay.

As they walked, Ava could hear birds singing in the tall trees overhead. The air was fresher and the river glistened in the sunlight. But there were also three police cars and an ambulance parked next to a barge. A police boat with blue flashing lights was moored behind it. A small group of people was sitting on the ground under a tree across from the barge. Access to the area was restricted by police tape that blocked off a large part of the quay.

Ava eyed Jaspar. He didn't have to speak for her to know that they were both thinking the same thing... *Whatever had gone wrong had gone very wrong.*

Pale, Jaspar took a deep breath and strode up to the policewoman standing at the wooden sawhorse barrier. "I'm Jaspar Porter, the producer of the film shooting on the barge. This is Ava Sext, my assistant. Nate Rosier, the production manager, called and asked us to come."

The police officer stepped away and spoke into a walkie-talkie that crackled loudly.

Jaspar pointed at the group of people under the tree. "That's some of the production crew, along with the lighting and decoration team. The dark-haired woman pacing back and forth chain-smoking is Claire, our assistant director.

The police officer walked back to them. "I need to see some identification."

Jaspar handed his passport to the policewoman. She glanced at it and returned it. She pulled back the tape and let them through.

As Jaspar and Ava walked down to the barge, a tall, fit man in his mid-thirties with solemn bearing and a steely look in his grey eyes strode toward them.

When he reached them, the man ran his fingers nervously

through his thick, dark hair. "Thank God, you're here."

Alarmed, Jaspar looked around. "Lance?"

The man raised his eyebrows. "He's at the production office. With luck, he won't appear." Noticing Ava for the first time, he stared at her.

Jaspar jumped in. "Introductions are in order. Ava Sext is going to work as my assistant. This is Nate Rosier, our production manager."

Ava studied Nate. He certainly didn't have the looks of a Casanova. If anything, he was very ordinary looking. He had grey eyes, thick dark hair and was dressed in jeans and a T-shirt. However, he exuded energy. When he spoke, you could feel the power and intensity of his personality.

"What happened to your assistant in London?" Nate asked with a side glance at Jaspar.

"Martin," Jaspar replied. "Now will you tell me what's going on?"

Nate looked back at the barge. "I have bad news."

Fear streaked across Jaspar's face. "What is it?"

"A dead man," Nate said. "On our barge!"

Stunned, Jaspar stepped backwards. "You're joking?"

Nate shook his head. "I'm afraid not. I was the first to arrive this afternoon. When I got here, the door to the interior of the barge was unlocked. I was angry. We'd left equipment inside. I was going to read the decorating crew the riot act. But the equipment was still there. So was a dead body."

Ava was too stunned to speak.

Jaspar went silent for a moment. "Is it a crew member?"

Nate looked surprised. "No. Just some man who went in, got drunk, fell and hit his head. The police found a bottle of whiskey next to his body."

"Can we shoot as planned?" Jaspar asked.

"I'm afraid not. The police are going to run a forensic investigation. Then we have to deal with the insurance company. Our insurance should cover any costs we incur," Nate said. "As long as one of us didn't kill the man, we're fine."

"That's not funny," Jaspar snapped.

"Gallows humor," Nate replied with a shrug.

"What did the man look like?" Jaspar asked.

Nate narrowed his eyes. "The dead man?"

Jaspar nodded and waited.

"I only looked at him for a few seconds before I closed the

door and called the police. I'd say he was in his fifties. Dark hair. He had blood on his face so I can't tell you much about that. Broken glasses were on the ground next to him. I didn't let any of the crew on the boat. The fewer people who have to deal with the police the better."

"What happens now?" Jaspar asked in a tone that showed he had regained control of his emotions.

"The police want to talk to the crew members who were on the boat yesterday. They want to talk to you and me. Simon came by after the police arrived. When he saw them, he didn't even come down the ramp. He just turned and left. It's good we aren't shooting as Mr. Too Busy To Do His Job didn't even stop by the barge yesterday to see the final changes."

"What did Simon say?" Jaspar asked, puzzled by the director's reaction.

Nate shrugged. "Simon was Simon. When I called him on his cell phone, he said it wasn't his problem. He's right in a certain way. He hasn't been to the barge in days. There's no reason for him to come now and deal with the police."

"We keep to our schedule?" Jaspar asked.

Nate was surprised by the question. "Of course. We have a film to make. Monday is the first day of principal photography. We'll start at the main set."

"But Ian won't be here until the end of the week. We need him for all the scenes that are shot there," Jaspar protested.

"We'll figure it out." Suddenly, Nate's eyes widened as he stared at something behind them. "It's Lance! You and Ava have to keep him away. If he starts talking to the police, he'll screw it up so badly we won't be able to shoot here for weeks!"

Jaspar wheeled around. Seeing Lance speaking to the policewoman, he spun toward Ava. "I'm going to need your help."

"What do you want me to do?" Ava asked as she glanced at the tall, thin man who was now walking toward them.

"I'm not sure yet. Let's go," Jaspar replied as he hurried toward Lance.

"If you can control him, we'll be fine," Nate said to Ava.

Viewing that as a challenge, Ava took a deep breath and strode off.

Lance LeGris was thin and wiry. Dressed in jeans and a light sweater, he had curly brown hair, an aquiline nose and hollow cheeks. He looked like a teenager, not a producer. Standing before them shaking and sweating, he was also a man on the edge of a nervous breakdown. "Claire told me that they found a dead man on our barge. What are we going to do? Was it murder?"

Jaspar put his hand on Lance's shoulder and smiled confidently. "Nate and I will deal with the police. We need you back at the production office. We're starting photography at the main set Monday evening."

Immense relief flooded over Lance's face. "You're sure you don't need me?"

"I'm positive," Nate responded.

Ava smiled and stepped toward Lance. "We haven't met. I'm Ava Sext, the new production assistant."

Puzzled, Lance eyed Jaspar. "What happened to your assistant in London?"

"Martin. She had enough of our irascible screenwriter," Jaspar explained. "Luckily, I discovered that Ava lives in Paris. We worked together on a film years ago."

As another police car drove down the quay with its lights flashing, Lance began to shake. "I knew something bad was going to happen."

Ava understood why Nate and Jaspar didn't want Lance to talk to the police. Who knows what he would blurt out in his mental state? He might even confess to the crime.

Jaspar grabbed Lance's arm and steered him toward the security perimeter. "Could you get Ava up to snuff on the film. She hasn't read the script and knows next to nothing about the production."

Wide-eyed, Lance looked at the police car. "Then I don't have to speak the police?"

"Nate and I will deal with everything," Jaspar insisted. "We need you at the office to get the ball rolling." Seeing something on the ground, Jaspar frowned and bent over.

"What is it?" Lance asked, terrified.

"The phosphorescent paint we used on the boat yesterday. Someone stepped in it. We'll have to clean it up or we'll have problems with the city," Jaspar said. "That's the last thing we need now."

CHAPTER 6

The taxi sped along the left bank of the Seine River toward the 6th arrondissement. Seated in the back seat, Ava eyed Lance who was staring out the window next to her. White-knuckled, he clutched the headrest of the seat in front of him. His brow was furrowed, and he appeared to be deep in thought. He hadn't said a word since they'd gotten in the taxi.

When the taxi stopped at a red light, Lance spoke to Ava in a wavering voice, "Did you see the body?"

Ava shook her head. "The only person who saw it was Nate. And the police, of course."

Hearing the word police, Lance began to shake. "Did Nate tell you what the dead man looked like?"

"Nate only saw him for a brief instant. The man was in his

fifties. He had dark hair. His face was covered with blood. He was on the floor. A bottle of whiskey was next to him."

Lance bit his lip. "What do the police think?"

"Nate didn't say," Ava responded. "I imagine it's too early."

"It's my fault," Lance announced. "I'm the French producer. We should have had a guard on the barge."

"To watch an empty boat? It was an accident. The man probably forced his way onto the barge to get drunk. He fell and hit his head. It's as simple as that," Ava said. As she spoke, she realized that it wasn't simple at all.

More worried than ever, Lance nodded. "You're right. It was an accident."

When the light turned green, the taxi sped off, and Lance fell silent again. Ava studied him. He was terrified. If there was a rabbit hole to hide in, he would have gone down it in a flash.

When the taxi crossed the Boulevard St. Michel, Lance leaned toward the driver. "Can you stop at the next corner? I don't feel well. I need to get out."

The driver slowed the taxi, crossed traffic and came to a halt. Lance paid him and stepped out onto the sidewalk. He was so upset, he could barely stand. He walked over to a building, leaned against it and slid down to the sidewalk, his head between his hands.

Ava got out of the taxi and joined him. "Are you OK?"

Lance shook his head. "If I said yes, I'd be lying. I feel horrible. The idea that someone died on my film is too awful to imagine. Things like that don't happen in real life."

"Accidents happen all the time. The man's death wasn't linked to the shoot. You aren't responsible," Ava said in an attempt to calm him.

Lance took a deep breath and looked up. "I was expecting something… Just not a death."

Ava wanted to ask what he was expecting, but she bit her tongue. She needed to gain Lance's trust before she started questioning him. "Are we far from the production office?"

Lance stood up and pointed to the corner. "The next street to the left."

They started walking. With each step, Lance's expression grew darker. At the corner, he stopped and turned to her.

"Nate's sure it wasn't one of the crew?" Lance asked.

"If it were, Nate would have recognized him," Ava responded gently. She understood why Jaspar had sent her to deal with Lance. He needed someone to get him through the crisis. "Look at the bright side. The accident happened before the shoot. The production has time to make other plans."

Lance didn't answer her. He turned left and walked down the street. At the cross street, he turned right. He walked a few feet and halted in front of a set of enormous coach doors on his left. He entered a code and pushed open a small door, cut into the center of one of the large coach door. He went through it. Ava followed him.

They were in an enormous courtyard paved with immaculate white stones. Low buildings lined both sides of the courtyard. A magnificent three-story private mansion rose between the low buildings. Tall trees and a garden were visible on the other side of the mansion through enormous glass windows that lined the mansion's ground floor.

"This is where you work?" Ava asked, astonished by the property's opulence.

"It belonged to my late uncle. The mansion was built in the 17th century. My uncle's father bought it after the war and restored it. The production office is over there," Lance said, pointing to a low building on their left. "It used to be the coach house."

As they walked toward the production office, an elegant woman dressed in a navy blue Chanel suit, dark stockings and gloves entered the courtyard. Large black sunglasses covered her face and a black wide-brimmed floppy straw hat hid her hair. A glass pendant swung as she walked. In the street, a black sedan sped off.

"It's my aunt," Lance told Ava. He hurried over to the woman and kissed her on both cheeks. Ava watched them speak. Lance's body language changed as he accompanied his aunt to the mansion's front door. As they spoke, he stood up straighter and appeared more confident. He opened the front door for his aunt and followed her into the mansion.

Seconds later, Lance came out. His gloom had lifted. He had a half-smile on his face. He strode over to Ava and beamed like a child who had just gotten a new toy for Christmas. "She said we can use the roof!"

"To film?" Ava asked, puzzled.

"Yes. Let me show you." Lance was so excited that he almost skipped to the mansion's front door. His anguish had been replaced by enthusiasm. "If I were directing the film, I'd use the roof for the establishing opening shot -- the sun rises over the garden."

Lance led her into the mansion. They were in a monumental entrance hall. The floor was tiled with black and white Italian marble. Gold gilt mirrors covered the hall's walls. On the right side of the entry, a sweeping stone staircase rose three floors. A gigantic crystal chandelier hung down from the ceiling. The crystals glittered in the afternoon sun.

Ava eyed a formal drawing room on her left. The room was decorated in a symphony of white and gold. Accent tones of rose, green and fuchsia were used for the drapes and throw pillows as well as the Oriental carpets that covered the parquet floor. Large vases of fresh flowers in the same tones of rose and fuchsia were on every table.

"It's beautiful," Ava said in awe.

"My aunt loves flowers," Lance replied. He walked over to the garden door, flung it open and stepped out into the garden.

Ava followed him outside. The garden was an oasis of beauty and calm in the middle of Paris. High stone walls encircled it. Centuries-old trees provided shade. Modern sculptures and enormous terracotta pots of flowers were scattered across the vast expanse of green grass. A small gazebo stood near the back wall.

Ava knew that Henri would approve of the mansion as it and its garden were hidden behind high walls and tall doors. Wealth was a taboo subject in France. The wealthier you were, the less you talked about it.

"I wish I had more time to spend here. But with the film, we're working around the clock. I shouldn't complain. A lot of people would like to be in my shoes," Lance said as he turned and walked back to the house.

Entering the hallway, Lance strode over to a small door in the wall. "We'll take the elevator up."

Ava was disappointed. She would have preferred to go up the

stairs and see what the upper floors hid. She stepped into the elevator behind Lance. He pressed a button, and the elevator rose silently. Looking down, he shook his head.

"What is it?"

"Some of the phosphorescent paint from the barge. I'd better clean it before my aunt sees it."

When the elevator doors opened on the top floor, they stepped out. They were in a long hallway. Doors lined both sides.

"These rooms used to be for the servants. At one time, a mansion like this would have had forty or fifty people working here. My aunt has a housekeeper and a cook, but they don't sleep on the premises," Lance said. "I'm not spitting on wealth. How could I? But having personnel at your beck and call seems very old-fashioned." He moved down the carpeted hallway and stopped at a door to the right. He turned the knob and pushed it open. The room was tiny. It was empty except for a telescope at the window and a round metal staircase that wound its way up to the ceiling.

Ava walked over to the telescope and peered through it. "The garden next door is even larger!" Ava exclaimed, surprised. Discovering one hidden garden in the center of Paris was surprising, discovering a second one was astonishing.

"That's the garden of our main set," Lance said. He pressed a button on the wall next to the metal staircase. There was a low sound of a motor kicking in, and a panel in the ceiling opened revealing the sky.

Ava was flabbergasted.

"Walk slowly, and hold the railing," Lance advised as he started up the metal stairs.

Ava went up the staircase behind Lance. When she stepped out onto a wooden platform on the roof, her breath was taken away. It had an incredible view of the neighborhood. "How did your uncle get permission to build this?"

Changes to historic buildings were regulated tightly by the city of Paris. A change like this to a 17th-century building would be nearly impossible. Many Parisians chaffed at the restriction and complained that Paris was a museum. As a Londoner, Ava appreciated that the old Paris hadn't been swept away by modern buildings. Walking through the center of Paris, you were linked to its past by the architecture. She imagined that someone walking through this neighborhood in one hundred years would see the same buildings Ava saw today.

"The German army requisitioned the building when they occupied Paris. They built this platform. When my grandfather bought the mansion, he was allowed to keep it." Lance pointed to the mansion at the end of the other garden. "We'll be shooting most of the film there."

Ava frowned. Jaspar had told her that the film had a low budget. Looking at the other mansion's well-groomed grounds, she sensed that an enormous amount of money was needed to keep them looking like that.

"We were really lucky. The mansion has been closed for years. When Nate had the idea of shooting there, he contacted the holding company that owns it, and they said yes. I couldn't believe it."

"You've been incredibly lucky," Ava replied.

Lance swallowed and smiled wanly. "Except for one dead body, and a screenwriter who's a nightmare."

Ava wondered when she'd meet the famous Martin Scotsdale. She had a feeling it would be sooner than she'd like.

They took the elevator down to the ground floor and walked through the entrance hall. They exited through the mansion's main doors and crossed over to the production office.

When they reached the coach house, Lance swung the door open. "Welcome to Catastrophe Productions!"

The minute Ava set foot inside, she could feel the mix of excitement, hard work, creativity and chaos that every film production office had. It was a heady mix. But today, she could also feel the weight of a dead body dragging things down.

Lance eyed the empty office, frowning. "Where is everyone?"

"Lance, look!" Ava said, pointing to a whiteboard.

Lance. Lunch is in the refrigerator. We're at the set.

Lance read the message and walked over to the refrigerator. He took out a large bag and peeked inside. "Sushi! Would you like to share lunch?"

"I'd love to, "Ava said. She wasn't hungry, but it was time to discover what was going on.

CHAPTER 7

Lance spread the food out on a table in the mansion's garden as Ava strolled around the bucolic setting. Overhead, birds were chirping. A white rabbit hopped across the immaculately groomed lawn. The flower beds were a riot of pink and red flowers. Ava's eyes moved from the moss-covered statue of a woman in the center of the lawn to the enchanting glassed-in gazebo surrounded by palm trees at its far end. Walking back toward Lance, she looked up at the mansion. A large French window on the upper floor was open. She sensed that someone was watching them. She wondered if it was Lance's aunt.

"There's sushi, sashimi, extra rice and soup," Lance said when Ava joined him. "What would you like?"

Despite having eaten lunch, Ava was inexplicably hungry

again. "I'll start with sashimi."

Lance served her and then took some sushi for himself. He settled into a dark green wrought iron chair across from Ava.

"Have you lived here long?" Ava asked, eying the mansion.

"Since last September. That's when I moved back to Paris from New York. The mansion had been empty for years as my aunt and uncle lived in Switzerland. My aunt returned here after his death last year. When she offered me a small apartment on the top floor, I accepted immediately."

"And now she's letting you use the former coach house as a production office," Ava said, dipping her salmon sashimi in soy sauce.

Lance nodded. "If we had to pay for a production office, our budget would be even more squeezed than it already is."

Ava waved her hand at the garden. "If I were your aunt, I'd spend all my time out here."

"I've never seen my aunt in the garden. But then I rarely see her. She's a very private person. The first time I met her was at my uncle's funeral," Lance said.

Ava's face showed her astonishment.

Lance sighed. "My family isn't close-knit. My parents moved to an ashram in India when I was a child. I grew up in boarding schools. Summers were spent at summer camp or with family friends. My only other relative was my uncle. I rarely saw him, although he was very generous financially. He paid for my education."

Ava opened the bottle of mineral water and poured them each a glass. "Jaspar told me you studied film at New York University."

Lance's face lit up. "I studied acting and directing there. I loved it. I loved New York. It's full of energy. You never knew what was going to happen."

"And now you're a film producer," Ava said.

Lance sighed heavily. "That was an accident. I wanted to make two short films that I wrote. It's every film student's dream. I couldn't find a production company in France to make them, so I opened my own company. My aunt lent me the money and the coach house. I owe her a lot. No, I owe her everything."

"How did you get involved with this film?" Ava asked.

"*Death on the Quai*? It was completely out of the blue. A lawyer called me. His client had a book that he wanted made into a film. They offered me incredible conditions to produce it. I couldn't refuse. Especially since my short films didn't open the doors that I hoped they would."

"Why did the lawyer choose your production company?" Ava asked as she hesitated between the tuna sashimi and the nigiri sushi.

Lance shook his head. "That's the million-dollar question. The film is about a jewel heist. My late uncle was a world-famous jeweler. Maybe the person financing the film thought that I'd have some insight into the subject." Lance laughed. "I don't."

Ava changed her mind and took a piece of salmon sashimi. She popped it into her mouth. It was excellent. It would be even better with a fruity white wine to accompany it.

"I never had anything to do with my uncle's business," Lance said. "I couldn't tell a ruby from a garnet."

Ava sipped her water. "How did you get involved with Silver Screen Productions?"

"Jaspar's company? Working with him was part of the deal... Just as Simon and Martin were. For the rest, we're free to do what we want."

Silent, Ava frowned. She hadn't learned anything that shone light on what was going on.

Lance crooked his head to the side. "I know what you're thinking. Something is wrong. I was so happy at the beginning that I didn't worry about the conditions that came with the money. Lots of backers insist on casting family or friends... Why not Simon and Martin? Maybe the backer knew them. Maybe he'd worked with them before. It's a vanity project. Vanity projects don't operate under the same criteria that regular projects do. I'm glad that the backer insisted on Silver Screen Productions though."

Ava was puzzled. "Why?"

"Because Jaspar knows what he's doing. He was the one who hired Nate." Lance smiled. "I have about as much insight into jewel heists as I do in dealing with screenwriters and directors."

"They're that bad?" Ava asked.

"When you meet Simon, you'll understand. He's either super-involved or missing in action. There's no middle ground with him. Some days, we don't see him. Other times, he's overzealous. Last night, for example, he was the last person working in the office when I left at ten thirty. He's also moody. He can be arrogant and dismissive. Then seconds later, he's utterly charming. I've never met Martin. Jaspar, Nate and Jaspar's assistant in London deal with him," Lance said as he served them both some California rolls. "They all say he's impossible."

"Is Martin arriving tomorrow?" Ava asked as she bit into her California roll. Sushi purists believed that California rolls were an abomination, but Ava loved the mix of avocado, surimi and sesame seeds.

"So it seems... Whether he arrives or not, we need the end of the film," Lance said, suddenly stressed.

"Wasn't the end in the book?" Ava asked.

"No. The book had an open end. A barge on the Seine blows up. We don't know who was on it. We don't know who was responsible for the explosion. We don't even know who has the jewel. We have no idea who lives or who dies. That's not a good ending for a film."

Ava frowned. "It's strange the writer didn't write a clear ending."

"I agree. The story also focuses on a love triangle. Two men and a woman. We have no idea what happens to those relationships. Does the woman stay with one of the men or both? Does she betray them? Does she die in the explosion? We don't know. That's what we're waiting for Martin Scotsdale to tell us."

"What do you know about the book's author?" Ava asked.

"Nothing. Absolutely nothing. Alan Smith is a very common name. There are millions of Alan Smiths in the world. The writer only wrote one book. We should probably thank our lucky stars for that, or we'd be producing a second horrible film after this one. In one month, shooting will be over. I'll be relieved when we reach the post-production phase. There's less that can go wrong there," Lance said

Ava was delighted by the opening that Lance had given her. "Jaspar said that strange things were going on."

Lance narrowed his eyes as he ate the last piece of sushi. "Strange? I wouldn't say that. We had some photos go missing. I'm convinced that it was a technical problem or an accident. Someone hit delete and doesn't want to admit it. As for the printed photos going missing, the only person who saw them was a woman who quit. And they weren't even for our film. They were from her last film. Since then, everything has gone smoothly."

Except for a dead body, Ava thought.

"I want the film to be a success so my aunt will be proud of me. I owe her that," Lance said in a sudden burst of passion.

"What did you mean when you said you expected something to go wrong on the film?" Ava asked as she and Lance piled the empty plates up.

"It has to do with me. I'm a bit of a jinx," Lance admitted. Lance's phone rang. He eyed the number. "It's Jaspar." Lance answered and listened. "Yes, Ava's here. OK. I'll meet you there." Lance hung up.

"What happened down at the barge?" Ava asked.

"The police have finished with the crew for today. I'm going to meet Jaspar and Nate at the set. Simon, of course, is nowhere to be found. Jaspar wants me to give you a script and the book. He'll see you at 9:30 tomorrow morning if you haven't changed your mind," Lance said as he smiled at her. "I hope you don't. We'll need all hands on deck to make it through the shoot."

CHAPTER 8

EXT. BARGE/SEINE RIVER - NIGHT

Night. Everything is plunged in darkness. The barge is barely visible in the blackness that surrounds it. The quay behind the barge is even darker. A figure makes its way across the dark quay. We can't tell if it's a man or a woman. The figure steps cautiously onto the barge's deck and halts as if listening for something. Then the figure moves slowly to the door and puts a gloved hand on it and pushes it opens.

A deafening explosion.

Shots of the explosion in the night sky.

Shots of debris burning on the water.

Fade to Black.

Sitting in her lawn chair in front of her stand on the Quai Malaquais, Ava turned to the next page in the script. It was blank. The remaining pages in the script were also blank.

As Lance had said, there was no end to the story.

Frustrated, she paged through the script from the beginning, rereading bits and pieces of it. From her prior film experience, she understood that scripts were blueprints for the director and the actors. A script was not intended to be a literary masterpiece. However, it did need to give the reader a clue as to who the characters were and why they were doing what they were doing.

This script did none of that.

Clearly, Martin Scotsdale had not been hired for his talent as a screenwriter. There must be some reason that the mysterious backer had insisted on hiring him. From Jaspar's description of Martin, it wasn't because of his human qualities.

With a sigh, Ava closed the script.

Tomorrow, she would meet Martin Scotsdale and discover the end of the story... if he had written it. Ava suspected that might not be the case. As Jaspar's assistant in London had dealt with Martin, Ava suspected that that role in Paris would fall to her.

"How's the film career going?" a voice said, startling her.

Ava looked up. Ali was standing next to her with a sketchpad in his hand.

"Henri told you?" Ava asked.

"There are no secrets, large or small, between booksellers," Ali joked. "Especially when it concerns Ava Sext and the good-looking Jaspar Porter."

"He is good-looking," Ava said with a smile. "And talented!"

Ali plucked the script from her lap and eyed its cover. "*Death on the Quai*. That's not the catchiest title."

"I'm not even sure there is a death as the script doesn't have an end," Ava complained.

"That is odd," Ali said, paging through it. "Some directors film different endings and do audience tests to choose one. But I've never heard of a film with no ending."

"Shooting multiple endings is prohibitively expensive unless it's a big American film," Ava said. "We have a tiny budget, an even smaller crew, two main sets, three main actors and a few secondary roles. We'll be lucky to film one ending, let alone several."

Ali shook his head with an amused smile on his lips. "It never fails…"

Ava eyed him, confused.

"You've been working on the film one afternoon, and already

you're using the royal "we"," Ali teased.

Ava smiled. "You're right. There's something addictive about film production. You quickly become part of a team."

Ali stopped at a page and read a scene out loud:

"EXT. BACK GARDEN/ MANSION -- NIGHT.

George creeps across the lawn. He looks up. In an upper window of the mansion, he sees Matt kissing Ella. Stunned, George freezes, unable to take his eyes off the scene. He takes a step forward, hesitates, turns and hurries back across the garden. He vanishes into the darkness."

Ava shook her head. "Claptrap! Complete claptrap!"

Ali raised his eyebrows. "I don't know. It could be interesting. It depends on the rest. Who's George?"

"A jewel thief," Ava responded, annoyed that Ali hadn't agreed with her.

"And Matt?"

"His accomplice."

The corner of Ali's eyes crinkled up. "Let me guess. Ella is George's girlfriend, and Matt is George's best friend."

Ava looked surprised. "How did you know that?"

"That's the way life works. The girlfriend always leaves with the best friend," Ali said with a knowing look on his face.

Ava looked stricken. "I'm sorry. I didn't know," she said with diplomacy. Ali rarely spoke about his private life. Now, she had stumbled onto what must have been a painful incident.

Seeing the expression on her face, Ali burst out laughing. "I wasn't talking about me. I'm not a jewel thief. In heist films, the love triangle is a familiar trope."

Ava was relieved that Ali was joking. In the last year, Ava had lost two boyfriends. Although she was a "live and let live" type of woman, she would be livid if either of them had left her for her best friend or even a casual acquaintance.

Ali continued to read. "What makes the situation especially gripping is the financial aspect."

Ava frowned. *Gripping?* Were they talking about the same script?

"The jewel heightens the intrigue," Ali said with enthusiasm. "We French are obsessed with money and love. Put them together, and the situation becomes explosive."

"Henri would agree with you. Henri's solution to every case is to follow the money or the love interest... or both," Ava said from experience.

"Henri is a wise man."

"Where is he? I had lunch with him. He didn't mention any appointments," Ava said, looking at his shuttered stand.

"He's off following the money," Ali explained.

"On my case?"

"How many other cases are there at the moment?"

Ava was delighted. Henri was an excellent sleuth. She had no doubts that he would dig up some useful information.

Ali paged through the script again, stopping here and there. "What if Ella was betraying both men? Seducing both men was her way to get the jewel."

"That doesn't make her a very sympathetic character," Ava said with disapproval.

"But it makes for an interesting story," Ali insisted.

Ava shook her head. "It destroys the love angle."

"It heightens the betrayal and makes Ella the master of her own destiny!" Ali countered.

Ava didn't like the idea that Ella was betraying both men. It ran counter to Ava's romantic streak. "Why would she use them to get to the jewel?"

"Use? That's a rather sexist reading of the situation. Let's just say that she wants the jewel and is ready to do what is necessary to get it. Don't forget that the jewel doesn't belong to the men. It's stolen," Ali reminded her.

"We'll know the end tomorrow," Ava said. "The screenwriter is bringing the last pages."

"Why doesn't he send them by email?" Ali asked, puzzled.

"If he did that, there would be no dramatic tension… Will the screenwriter write the end or not?" Ava replied, tongue in cheek.

Ali shook his head. "He should have found the end before he wrote the script."

"Why?" Ava asked, puzzled. "He waited until the end because he knew the characters better."

Ali nodded. "Point taken. But by the time you've reached the end, you've already made decisions that narrow your options. Take my paintings, for example. I decide what I want to paint. But each brush stroke narrows my options and leads to the next stroke. If I don't know where I'm going at the beginning, I'll end up with a completely different painting from the one I wanted to paint. I imagine it's the same way in a book."

Ava pursed her lips, unconvinced.

"I can see you don't agree with me."

"Convince me," Ava said with a light smile.

"Martin has created a set up that narrows the possible

endings," Ali said.

"What do you see happening?"

Ali balanced back on his heels. "Matt is attracted to Ella. Once George and Ella start seeing each other, Matt can't ask her out without betraying his best friend. If Ella dates Matt without telling George then she is betraying the man she supposedly loved. So we have two betrayals. Once you reach that point, your options narrow. Life isn't all unicorns and rainbows. There's no turning back from a betrayal like that. George can kill both of them and take the jewel. He can kill Matt and take the jewel. Or Matt and Ella could kill George and take the jewel. I like the solution where Ella takes the jewel and lets Matt and George kill each other... It's more modern."

Bewildered, Ava shook her head. "Stick to painting, Ali. What you said makes no sense."

"Don't you find it curious that your film is called *Death on the Quai*, and there was a death on the Quai Henri IV today?"

Ava's face lit up. "The dead body on the Quai Henri IV was my dead body. I mean Jaspar's and mine!"

"Your dead body?" Ali said, eyeing Ava with concern.

"Not my dead body. The production's dead body. It was found on a barge that is a shooting location for the film!"

"Wow! So you did have a death on the quay after all," Ali said

82

with real enthusiasm.

"It's a coincidence!" Ava said.

"It might be linked to the barge and not your film," Ali said.

Ava's eyes widened. "What?"

"That barge is supposedly cursed," Ali explained. "Years ago, it caught on fire and almost sank. Every now and then, lights are seen in it even when no one is there."

"How do you know that?"

"I was sketching down by the river patrol dock. One of the officers told me about it. He heard it from his former captain who was on duty when the boat caught on fire years ago."

Ava's every sense was on alert. That the dead man died on a haunted boat that was cursed was not a coincidence. She didn't know what it meant, but she intended to find out.

CHAPTER 9

Ava took a sip of white wine and turned the page in *Death on the Quai*. The book was even more bare-boned than the script. For the life of her, she couldn't understand why anyone would invest money to adapt the book to the big screen even if the person backing the film had written it. But that could be said about many books that were made into films. Maybe it was part of the mystery of cinema.

Looking up at the cloudless sky, Ava smiled. The rainstorm that morning was already a distant memory. It was a perfect summer evening. It was almost 9 p.m., and the sun was still high in the sky. The sun would be up until a little after 10. While Paris might not be the land of the midnight sun, summer days were long.

Taking advantage of the rare conjuncture of a long day and

good weather, Ava was seated on the outdoor terrace of an iconic bistro on the rue Bonaparte where she and Henri were meeting for dinner. Although after two lunches Ava wondered if she should eat again. She quickly discarded the thought. Everyone needs to have dinner.

As she sipped her wine, Ava gazed around the bistro's crowded terrace. Next to her, trendily dressed art dealers from the neighboring galleries were talking shop. A few tables down, some collectors were eying works on their phones while drinking an expensive bottle of Chablis. Young artists from the nearby Beaux Arts Academy were standing around a table on the sidewalk nursing their beers as they chatted loudly. Tourists, delighted to have found an authentic Paris bistro with real Parisians, were scattered about soaking up the atmosphere.

Ava wondered if she counted as a real Parisian yet. She suspected that no matter how long she lived in Paris, her London quirkiness would always be present, surfacing when she least expected it. Popping an olive into her mouth, she settled back in her chair.

When Henri had texted her suggesting dinner at the bistro, she had immediately accepted. She had so much to tell him, and she imagined he had a lot to tell her. In fact, she was dying to get his take on what was going on.

Ava chided herself.

Dying was not the most appropriate term to use on a day that some unfortunate soul had turned up dead.

After her conversation with Ali, Ava's first thought had been to call Jaspar and ask him how they had chosen the barge. She had decided against it, just as she had decided against walking past the set. If the choice of the barge was part of some nefarious plan, she didn't want anyone to know that she was on to them until she knew what was going on. The only thing she was sure of was that something was going on

She hadn't decided whether the death on the barge was an accident or a murder. She didn't believe in cursed barges anymore than she believed in haunted mansions. There must be more of a back-story than Ali had told her.

Ava took another sip of her wine. It was white Bordeaux from the Pessac-Léognan region. It had hints of citron and white flowers. It would have gone perfectly with her sushi lunch. Even without sushi, the wine was a wonderful start to the evening.

She turned her attention back to *Death on the Quai*. The book and the script were almost identical. However, there was one major difference. The book's author had been very vague about the relationship between Ella and the two men.

In the script, Martin made it clear that Ella was seeing both George and Matt. The book hinted that Ella was attracted to both men and that the men were attracted to her. But it had left it at that.

Did Ella have a relationship with one or both of the men?

The book didn't tell you that.

If a relationship did exist, what was it based on? Was it love, lust or just a means to get the jewel as Ali had suggested. Again, it was impossible to tell from the book.

Ava's opinion of Martin had gone up after reading the book. He had not copied/pasted as she had believed. He had developed the characters. Ava wondered why he had chosen to make the love trio central to the story.

Thinking back to the script, she tried to see things from Ella's point of view. What was Ella's role in the heist? Was she only a passive participant or was she acting as a free agent with her own agenda? If she was a passive participant, why did she stay when she realized the men were going to steal a jewel? Why didn't she protest or leave?

Ava disagreed with Ali's take on Ella's character: Ella was not a *séductrice*, a man-eater, who was out for the jewel.

Ava saw Ella as an independent woman who happened to fall in love with two men at the same time.

Yes, both men happened to be jewel thieves... but that could happen to anyone.

Ava tried to imagine what she would do if she were in Ella's shoes. If Ava got involved in a heist, it would be for love, not money. But then you never knew what you would do until you did it.

"I ordered some salmon rillettes to start with," Henri said as he slid into a seat across from Ava. He eyed the book and the script on the table. "You read them?"

"Both of them. You'll see. There's not much to read. Even as scripts go, the script is basic. The book is even more devoid of details," Ava complained.

"Won't that give the director more artistic leeway?" Henri asked.

"Perhaps," Ava said. "But as a producer, I'd like to know what film I'm making…"

"What happened on the set?" Henri asked disingenuously.

Ava raised an eyebrow. "You know what happened. I can tell from the way you asked the question. A body was found on the barge."

"I meant what happened when you and Jaspar arrived on the quay." Henri signaled for the waiter. "Two glasses of champagne and bring a cheese platter along with the rillettes."

"Champagne?" Ava asked, astonished.

Henri nodded. "To celebrate your return to film. Now tell me what happened on the quay."

"When we got there, the police had already cordoned off the area. Immediately, Jaspar and I knew something was very wrong. Then Nate, the production manager, told us about finding the body."

"The production's Casanova?" Henri asked.

Amused, Ava cocked her head to the side. "Casanova? I was disappointed. I had expected someone incredibly handsome. Nate was ordinary looking. Although you could tell he was focused and intelligent."

"That's the most dangerous type of Casanova," Henri said.

Ava looked puzzled. "Why do you say that?"

"Women don't have their guard up!"

The waiter brought over two glasses of champagne.

Henri took his glass and raised it in the air. "To Ava, my partner-in-crime."

Ava smiled and raised her glass in the air. "Let's just say, crime-solving partner!"

They clinked glasses.

As Ava sipped her champagne, she made a mental note of what Henri had said. She would keep her guard up around Nate to avoid being swept under his spell. Jaspar on the other hand… Ava would be delighted to fall under his spell. She hoped the feeling was mutual.

"Did Nate know the man?" Henri asked.

"The dead man? He'd never seen him," Ava said.

"What did the dead person look like?" Henri asked as he sipped his champagne.

"Nate said he was in his fifties. His face was covered with blood. Nate believes he slipped and hit his head. There was a bottle of whiskey on the floor next to him."

Henri frowned. "How did he get into the barge?"

"The door might have been forced," Ava said.

"But someone might have left it unlocked…" Henri suggested.

"That's a possibility," Ava said. "Film shoots get crazed."

"And the shoot Monday night?" Henri asked.

"They can't shoot on the barge until the police finish their investigation. The production is moving to the main set," Ava said. "Ali learned something interesting."

The waiter arrived with bread, salmon rillettes, a cheese platter, two wine glasses and a bottle of the same white Bordeaux Ava had been drinking earlier. He put everything in the center of the table and poured wine into the glasses. He removed the champagne glasses and left.

"How are we going to eat all of this?" Ava asked, eying the feast on the table.

"Slowly," Henri said as he took a piece of bread and spread some salmon rillettes on it. "What did Ali tell you?"

"The barge caught fire years ago and almost sank."

Henri's eyes widened. "The same barge?"

Ava nodded. "The same barge..."

"That can't be a coincidence," Henri said.

"Ali said some of the river police told him the boat is cursed."

"Cursed is a strong term to use," Henri said, narrowing his eyes. "Haunted brings us back to the main set, and I don't believe in ghosts."

"I've never met a ghost, so I can't say one way or the other."

Henri burst out laughing.

"We'll have to find out why people think that the main set is haunted," Ava insisted.

"What else did you learn?" Henri asked.

"I met the owner of Catastrophe Productions, Lance LeGris," Ava replied with a twinkle in her eye.

Henri raised his eyebrows. "And?"

"Catastrophe Productions is aptly named. Lance is like the captain of a sinking ship. He's in way over his head. Jaspar and Nate tasked me with keeping Lance away from the quay. I had lunch with him in his aunt's garden. She lives in the most incredible 17th-century mansion. It's impossible to believe that a mansion like that exists in the heart of Paris. I didn't get to meet the director. Lance, like Jaspar, described him as making the film for the money."

"Good for him!" Henri said.

Ava was startled.

"Creative people often work for love and not money. You can love what you're doing, but you should get paid for it. Those are Ali's words, but I agree," Henri said.

Suddenly hungry, Ava took a piece of goat's milk cheese that was shaped like a flattened pyramid and bit into it. She washed it down with a sip of white wine.

"There's an interesting story behind that cheese," Henri said.

"The Valençay?" Ava asked.

Henri nodded. "Originally, the cheese was shaped like a pyramid. When Napoleon returned to France after an unsuccessful expedition to Egypt, he saw the cheese and was so angry that he lopped off the top with his sword. Ever since then, it's had a flat top."

"That could be a film!" Ava said, enchanted by the story.

"And the infamous screenwriter?" Henri asked.

"Martin Scotsdale is arriving tomorrow. At least, he's supposed to arrive. Lance hasn't met him yet and isn't looking forward to it." Ava pointed at the script. "Martin's bringing the end of the script with him. Both the book and the script end with the boat exploding. You never know what happened to the characters or the jewel," Ava said as she took a sip of wine. "Your turn."

Henri sat back in his chair. "My turn... I was intrigued by the LeGris connection. Louis LeGris was a jeweler to the wealthy and famous for years. He catered to the jet set at a time when air travel was for the very rich. He had shops in Paris, Monte Carlo and Hong Kong. He dated famous actresses. He made his fortune at a time that it was easier to evade taxes. Although, the LeGris family has always been rich."

"Lance said his parents moved to India when he was a child and sent him to boarding school," Ava said.

Henri sighed. "His parents essentially abandoned him. They gifted their money to an ashram. Lance's uncle paid for his schooling. But you know that."

"When did Mr. LeGris leave Paris? Lance said the mansion had been closed since Mr. LeGris moved to Switzerland."

"Thirty years ago, LeGris closed his shop in Paris, moved to Zurich and got married. It was a private ceremony. His jet set life was over. He was in his sixties so maybe it was time to settle down. He still sold high-end jewelry to millionaires, but he gave up the nightclub circuit and all the rest. To people who knew him before, it all seemed very mysterious. No one knew his wife."

"How did you learn this?" Ava asked.

"I spoke to his father's notary, Maître Medon," Henri said.

Ava was astonished. "He's still alive?" If Mr. LeGris died last year at ninety-two that means his father would be at least one hundred and twelve if he were alive today. So his notary would be even older."

Henri laughed. "Don't you know notaries live forever? Maître Medon's grandfather was the older Mr. LeGris's notary. Maître Medon took over from his grandfather when he was a mere thirty."

Ava should have figured out the situation. Notarial offices often stayed in the family. They went from father to son or grandson. Henri had sold his practice to his nephew, also a DeAth. "And the inheritance?"

"The grandfather had property and owned sugar plantations

abroad. He was the biggest sugar importer in France after the war. His inheritance was divided evenly between his two sons. His oldest son was Louis LeGris. When Lance's grandfather was 80, he married again and had Lance's father. There was a huge age difference between the two brothers. The older brother inherited the mansion."

"Who inherited it when he died?" Ava asked as she put some salmon rillettes on a piece of bread.

"His wife," Henri said. "No one knows anything about her except that Louis LeGris fell madly in love with her and remained that way until he died. Her name was Anne Dupont.... Maître Medon tried to find out more about her, but there are millions of Anne Duponts in France. Thirty years ago, people didn't have Facebook pages where they shared their lives."

"I met her!" Ava announced, excited.

Henri's eyebrows shot up. "Tell me everything."

"I only saw her for a few minutes. She was elegantly dressed in a Chanel suit. She had on huge dark glasses, a large hat and was wearing gloves."

"In July?" Henri asked.

"Lots of older women wear gloves year-round," Ava responded. "My great aunt is eighty-five and wouldn't be seen without them, winter or summer. Of course, she also believes that you don't wear white after August fifteenth."

"What was Madame LeGris doing?"

"Returning to the mansion. A black car dropped her off. I only saw her from afar," Ava said. "When she dies, who inherits her estate?"

Henri burst out laughing. "You're becoming more French than the French. Louis LeGris set up a trust and a foundation. After his wife's death, half of her fortune will go to the foundation and half will go to Lance... Unless she changes the terms of the trust which she has the right to do."

"How do you know that?" Ava asked. "Isn't that supposed to be confidential?"

Henri shook his head. "Trusts are registered. The rest is confidential. But Maître Medon is worried about her."

"Why?" Ava asked.

"He asked to meet her when she moved back to Paris. She refused. He suggested hiring a guard for the mansion or a driver. Again she refused. I promised him that if I discovered she was in danger, I would call him immediately. He's never met her which I think is odd."

"If she is in danger, it isn't from Lance. He adores his aunt," Ava said. "What if the dead man is linked to the LeGris family?"

"Then his death wouldn't be accidental," Henri said.

Ava's cell phone began to vibrate. She took it out and checked the number. "It's Jaspar!" She answered the call. "Jaspar! Lance said things went well with the police. That's a relief." She nodded as she listened. "I'm reading the script right now. Henri's number? You're in luck. He's sitting right across from me." Ava handed her cell phone to Henri.

Henri put the phone up against his ear. "Jaspar! How is your new assistant working out?" Henri listened and laughed.

Ava wished the phone was on speakerphone.

"Tomorrow at 9:45? I'll be there," Henri said. He ended the call and handed the phone back to Ava.

"What is it?" Ava asked.

In response, Henri signaled the waiter. "Two more glasses of champagne!"

"Champagne? Again? Jaspar's putting me in the film?" Ava asked.

Henri smiled. "No. He's putting me in the film. I'm going to be Ian Granger's double."

Ava was speechless.

CHAPTER 10

"Lights, camera, action!"

The sharp sound of a clap opening and closing. The camera began to film.

A wide shot of Ava standing next to the gazebo in the LeGris garden. The camera zoomed in on Ava's face as a spotlight bathed her in a blinding whiteness.

"I don't know who the murderer is," Ava protested, holding her right hand in front of her eyes.

The camera pulled back revealing Jaspar walking toward her. "You have to tell me who the murderer is before someone else dies," Jaspar begged.

A shot of Ava shaking her head. "I don't know who the murderer is."

A look of panic on Jaspar's face. "We need to discover the truth before it's too late."

The sound of a gunshot.

Jaspar gasped. He buckled over and fell to the ground. A pool of blood formed around his inert body.

"Jaspar!" Ava screamed.

Everything went dark.

A male voice echoed from the darkness. "Wherever you go, people die! You cause their deaths."

Wild-eyed, Ava looked around, desperately trying to discover where the voice was coming from. "That's not true. People do die, but I have nothing to do with their deaths. I'm only trying to solve the case."

The voice spoke again. "This is one case you won't be able to solve."

A shot rang out. Ava clutched her throat and fell to the ground.

A different male voice spoke. "Cut! You were great, Ava! It's too bad you're dead!"

Startled, Ava opened her eyes. The garden and Jaspar had vanished. Ava was alive. She was sitting in bed in her apartment. Sunshine was streaming through the overhead windows.

Ava was shaken. She had died in dreams before, but those deaths hadn't felt real. This time, her death had felt real. Trying to chase away the image of Jaspar's dead body and hers, Ava sat up and swung her legs over the side of the bed.

She checked the clock by the bed. It was still early. She had plenty of time to have a leisurely breakfast and get ready for her day at the production office. Given yesterday's events, she suspected that it would be a long day.

Standing up, she stretched and slipped her feet into her slippers and walked to the kitchen. She stopped in front of her uncle's record collection.

While yesterday had been a day for "Born to be Wild", today was different. Today, she needed music that would inspire her and help shake off her feeling of impending doom.

Instinctively, she chose the album *Surrealistic Pillow* by Jefferson Airplane. She closed her eyes and put the needle down on a song at random. The moment the first notes of "Somebody to Love" came on, Jaspar' face popped into her mind... a very alive Jaspar

Jaspar was like good wine. He had gotten better with age.

Buoyed by the music, she poured cat food into Mercury's bowl. When her furry meal mate arrived, his breakfast would be waiting for him.

Crossing the kitchen, she opened the refrigerator and took out a pitcher of hibiscus ice tea. She poured some into a glass and walked over to the large wooden table and sat down.

She opened her laptop and typed "dying in a dream" into the search engine. Her dream might mean nothing, or it might be incredibly important. The only way to know was to consult the search engine gods. Hundreds of thousands of results appeared.

She chose the first one:

Dying in a dream could be a good omen. It might also be a warning that something bad was about to happen.

That was called hedging your bets, Ava thought, annoyed at the imprecision of the analysis.

Undeterred, she typed in "being shot in a dream". She read through several results and stopped on one that appeared to encompass her situation:

If someone shoots you, you are experiencing danger in your life!

For Ava, that hit the nail on the head.

If the dead man had been killed because of the film, whoever killed him would not like someone poking around.

Luckily, Jaspar was the only person who knew that she was a sleuth. Somewhat reassured, she went to the bathroom to get ready.

She took a long hot shower. Afterward, she used all her favorite products. She put on her face cream and added a generous dollop of sunscreen. The one advantage of Paris's weather was that most of the year you didn't need to break the bank for sunscreen.

Pulling her hair back in a ponytail, she added a touch of blush and mascara.

Next step: wardrobe.

If choosing the right clothing for a character in a film was important, it was even more important in your daily life as your daily life was real.

She headed to the closet and eyed her clothing. After deciding against her favorite black lace top -- it was a film shoot, not a fashion show -- she chose a pair of jeans that were the perfect shade of blue, a dark blue cotton top, a navy blue sweater and dark blue sports shoes. She threw on a lime green leopard print chiffon scarf for a touch of color.

When she finished dressing, she went back to the bathroom and added some highlighter to her cheeks. She stepped back and scrutinized herself.

In her own humble opinion, she looked great.

She headed back to the kitchen and poured herself some more hibiscus tea. As she drank it, she felt eyes on her. Looking down, she saw Mercury staring up at her in disapproval.

"There's nothing wrong with a girl looking good."

Her words didn't assuage Mercury's doubts.

Ava sighed. The world was full of critics, even four-footed ones. She eyed the cat. "It might be a little over the top for a sleuth, but Jaspar is exceedingly good looking. Don't forget, Benji and I have agreed to move on."

Hearing Benji's name, Mercury meowed loudly.

Ava crouched down in front of the cat and stared in his eyes.

"Benji's not moving on from you. You are his favorite Parisian cat. You are probably his favorite cat in the whole world... When he comes back to Paris, he'll visit you. Benji and I aren't stopping our relationship. We're changing it. He and I will always be friends."

Somewhat assuaged, Mercury swung his tail and began to eat.

Ava stood up and stared down at him. *Men! They always stick together.*

"I'm off. Do the dishes before you leave!" Ava said with a breezy wave.

Mercury ignored her.

Ava had never had a cat, so she didn't know if cats were known for having a sense of humor. If that were the case, Mercury was an outlier. He didn't have a funny bone in his body.

At the door, Ava glanced at herself in the mirror one last time. Her look was missing something -- her secret weapon. She pulled a tube of red lipstick from her pocket, swiped it on and checked her image in the mirror.

Perfection!

Café Zola was empty. The early morning rush was over, and it was too early for lunch. Behind the counter, Gerard was writing the daily specials on the chalkboard.

Seeing Ava arrive, he stopped, acknowledged her presence with a curt nod and headed to the espresso machine. He made a double espresso. Turning, he handed it to Ava.

"What if I wanted a *café crème* today?" Ava asked as she unwrapped a sugar cube and dropped it in her cup.

"You'd get a double espresso," Gerard responded.

Ava peered into the kitchen. "Where's Alain?" Alain was Gerard's cousin and co-owner of the café. He was also the chef whose cooking was a feat of alchemy.

"He's out jogging," Gerard replied as he went back to the chalkboard.

In shock, Ava stared at Gerard. "Jogging? You mean running?"

Puzzled, Gerard looked up. "What other type of jogging is there?"

Ava tried to wrap her mind around the fact that Alain, the same Alain who spent all of his waking hours looking for the best cheeses and finest wines, was now running around somewhere in Paris.

"When did this happen?" Ava asked, alarmed.

Gerard knitted his brows together in false outrage. "For your information, we have lives outside the café. Café Zola is not a film set that you come to when you want a typical Parisian café."

"I didn't mean to offend you," Ava said, hoping she hadn't gotten on the bad side of the testy Gerard.

"I have a secret life that would shock you," Gerard said with a lascivious smile.

Ava was speechless.

Gerard burst out laughing. "I'm joking. You're right. I don't have a life outside the café. Neither does Alain. He just wants to stay fit. It's either running or doing chin-ups in the kitchen."

Pursing her lips, Ava wondered where this quest to stay fit would lead. Would the café start to serve lean cuisine? Not that there was anything wrong with lean cuisine except that Ava would miss Alain's *côte de boeuf.*

In an attempt to see which way the wind was blowing, Ava eyed the chalkboard. "What's the special today?"

"Duck confit with baby potatoes and a green salad," Alain replied.

"And dessert?" Ava asked.

"Baba au Rhum," Gerard mumbled as he wrote.

Reassured, Ava sipped her coffee. Her culinary haven was safe for now.

Gerard finished writing and propped the chalkboard up against the wall.

"Has Henri come by?" Ava asked.

With a suspicious look in his eye, Gerard turned and stared at her. "This early? Why would he do that?"

"I don't know," Ava said, not wanting to reveal that Henri was working on the film.

Aware she was hiding something, Gerard stared at her.

Ava avoided his eyes. "Where's the newspaper?"

Gerard strode to the far end of the bar and brought it over.

Ava read the headline that was splashed across the front page. It wasn't "Death on the Quai Henri IV" as she had expected. It read "American Fashion Idol Robbed of Jewels at Gunpoint". In disbelief, Ava scanned the article. In fact, the first five pages of the paper were devoted to the story. There were photos of the star wearing the stolen jewels. There were eyewitness accounts by anyone who had been in the vicinity of the site of the robbery. There were several articles lamenting safety in Paris. There was nothing about a death on a barge on the Seine.

Gerard pointed at the front page. "It gives Paris a bad name when people are robbed here. She should have stayed home."

Ava thought of arguing with him but decided against it. Gerard loved Paris. Born and raised in the city, he was its most fervent defender.

Ava paged through the paper. Halfway through it, she found a short article about a death on a barge. There were few details. The journalist wrote that the police believe the death was an accident.

Cheered by this stroke of good fortune, Ava took a croissant out of the basket on the zinc countertop and bit into it. Catastrophe Production had lucked out again. Lance was the luckiest jinx around. The robbery of the American fashion star had completely eclipsed Ava's murder.

Correction... the production's murder.

Ava was astonished that she was now referring to the death as a murder. There was no evidence that it was anything other than an accident. But her sleuthing sixth sense was telling her that it was a murder.

"How's your film career going?" Gerard asked.

Ava was surprised. "Henri told you?"

"Why wouldn't he tell me? Café Zola was in a film six years ago. The murderer had a coffee right where you're standing."

Instinctively, Ava moved to the left.

"I served the killer his coffee. They cut me out during the final edit," Gerard said with a sigh of true disappointment. He added with a knowing look, "Jaspar seems like a nice guy."

Ava stopped eating her croissant, mid-bite. *How did he know Jaspar's name?*

Reading her thoughts, Gerard raised his eyebrows. "Waiters know everything that's going on around them. We're not deaf and dumb."

Ava suspected he had noticed her attraction to Jaspar. "Jaspar and I knew each other when we were young."

Gerard cracked a smile. "And now you're both in your dotage?"

Ava laughed.

"Should I save you and Jaspar the special of the day," Gerard asked. "Or will you be working on the film with Henri?"

Ava eyed Gerard. He was full of surprises today. "Henri only learned he was in the film last night! How do you know that?"

"He texted me to cancel his duck confit," Gerard explained.

Suddenly, Ava stared at Gerard. "What else did you notice about Jaspar?"

Gerard thought for a moment before answering. "He looked like he was expecting bad news,"

Ava was stunned. *Did Jaspar know about the body when he came to the café for lunch?*

Gerard eyed the sunlight that was streaming into the café and shook his head. "If the weather keeps up like this, I'll be working in shorts."

Ava burst out laughing. "Pigs will have wings before that happens."

CHAPTER 11

Ava left Café Zola and hurried down the quay to the production office. While a few booksellers had already opened their stands, there was no sign of Ali or his brother, Hassan. If Ava weren't working on the film, she'd be opening her stand right now. Given the weather, she might even have worn shorts.

Despite the death on the barge, she was excited. Working on a film was a heady experience. Working on a film where something criminal might be taking place was exciting. Working on a film where something criminal might be taking place, a crime that she and Henri had been asked to investigate, was even more exciting... and challenging.

As she walked, her mind went back to something that Henri had mentioned at dinner the night before: Louis LeGris's sudden departure from Paris. From one day to the next, Mr. LeGris had closed his mansion, shuttered his Parisian store and given up his jet setting ways to lead a quiet life in Switzerland.

Why had he done this? What was behind this drastic change in lifestyle?

Ava was a firm believer that people could change at any age. Henri and her late Uncle Charles were proof of that. Still, Louis LeGris's abrupt transformation from jet-setter to near recluse struck her as odd.

As the French would say: "*il y a anguille sous roche*" -- there's an eel under the rock. Ava couldn't help but smile at the reaction her English friends would have if she started talking about eels under rocks. Some French expressions didn't translate well. The expression meant that something smelled fishy.

No matter what the language, there was definitely something fishy or "eely" about LeGris's sudden departure.

But what?

Mr. LeGris might have been ill and moved to Switzerland for the air. The proof -- he lived to a ripe old age.

Or he might have been fleeing someone. If that were the case, Switzerland seemed a poor choice of a place to hide. It was close enough to France to get there in a few hours, and LeGris's presence in the country hadn't been a secret. If Ava were on the lam, she'd go to a remote island in the Pacific or an isolated village in the Brazilian rain forest, not Switzerland.

It was also possible that LeGris was insanely jealous and wanted to keep his new wife to himself. Ava tried to imagine Madame LeGris held prisoner on a Swiss mountaintop. It didn't gel with the woman Ava had seen. Although she had only observed Madame LeGris for a few minutes, she appeared to be a woman who was very much in control.

Still, it was strange that Lance had never met her before the funeral.

Ava made a mental note to learn more about the mysterious Madame LeGris.

Ava left the quay and made her way to the production office. When she turned onto the street where it was located, long rows of orange and white traffic cones lined the curb, blocking all the parking spots. Flyers were taped to the streetlights.

Ava stopped and read one:

Catastrophe Productions and Silver Screen Productions have the authorization of the Paris Prefecture of Police to reserve and use parking spaces for the production of the film "Death on the Quai". All taxes and fees have been paid.

Several official stamps dotted the bottom of the authorization form.

Reading the flyer, Ava felt excitement bubble through her.

The shoot was on!

She had feared that it might be canceled because of the death.

The flyer meant that Monday afternoon, the huge trucks that carried the lighting equipment, cameras and electric generators would park where the cones were, and filming would begin.

The film she had worked on with Jaspar had been a short film shot with a handheld camera. It didn't have a professional crew or professional equipment.

Despite its low budget, *Death on the Quai* was a real film.

With a real death, Ava reminded herself.

She advanced to the LeGris mansion's large coach doors. She entered the code and stepped into the courtyard. Everything was silent. No one was visible. The mansion's shutters were all closed. Ava strode to the production office. Before she could reach it, she heard a noise behind her. Turning, she saw Lance walking toward her.

"You're early!" Lance said as he opened the unlocked door and stepped into the office.

Ava eyed Lance. His face was drawn. There were dark shadows under his eyes. His clothing was rumpled and looked like it had been slept in.

"I was worried you wouldn't come back after yesterday!" Lance said in a falsely upbeat tone.

"I don't scare easily," Ava responded.

Lance wrung his hands nervously together. "I didn't sleep all night. We're off to a bad start. I'm waiting for the next shoe to drop."

"Every production has its challenges. Francis Ford Coppola went temporarily blind while filming *Apocalypse Now*, and the German director Werner Herzog was almost killed while filming *Fitzcarraldo* in the Amazon," Ava said in a bid to be reassuring.

Lance's eyes widened in horror, and his jaw dropped.

Seeing his reaction, Ava winced. "Sorry. I just meant that in the grand scheme of things everything is going relatively well on this film."

"Other than a dead body," Lance responded with a forced grin.

"The newspaper said it was an accident," Ava replied.

Lance nodded. "You're right. I need to look at the bright side. Imagine what our lives would be like if the American star hadn't been robbed. We'd have the press camping out on our doorstep." He walked over to the snack table. "Coffee?"

"I thought you'd never ask," Ava replied.

"I got here early to make it. Good coffee makes all the difference," Lance said as he poured them each a cup.

"You're a man after my own heart," Ava said in approval. She took her cup and sipped it. Lance hadn't lied. The coffee was great.

"I see I've arrived in the nick of time," Jaspar said as he entered the office and strolled over. He held up a bag. "I stopped by the bakery. We'll need a sugar rush to get us through the day."

Seeing Jaspar, Ava stood taller. Jaspar was charming. Dressed in jeans and a dark blue T-shirt, he was even better looking than yesterday. Her inner voice chided her: *This was no time for romance. She had a death to solve.*

Ava frowned.

Her inner voice had almost said "*deaths*"… as in more than one. Had her sleuthing sixth sense picked up on something that she had missed?

"Jaspar, we need to postpone the film," Lance said.

"That's out of the question," Jaspar replied as he poured himself a coffee."

"We had a man die on our barge," Lance protested.

"The police believe it was an accident," Jaspar said as he took croissants out of the bag.

"And the rest?" Lance said without specifying what the rest was.

Jaspar sipped his coffee. "It's too late to stop. If we don't shoot as planned, the film won't get made. We'll lose the actors, our main location, our backer and the money… Something Silver Screen Productions can't afford to do. The backer's lawyer called me last night. He'd heard about the death."

"How?" Lance asked as fear darted across his face.

"I didn't ask," Jaspar replied. "The lawyer was very clear. We have to start principal photography as planned or lose funding."

"Why didn't you call me?" Lance asked with growing panic.

Jaspar eyed the disheveled man before him. "If I had called you, you'd have gotten less sleep than you obviously got. Come on, Lance. Pull yourself together. We need to make the film. We're producers. That's what we do!"

"Morning all," a tall fit man in his mid-fifties said as he breezed in. Full of energy, he was dressed in a grey T-shirt with the name of a rock band on it, jeans and black motorcycle boots. Bald with chiseled features, he looked every inch the filmmaker. He was holding a script in his hand.

Ava guessed that this was the famous Simon Hepplewhite.

Lance shook his head in disapproval. "Why are you so upbeat? It's obscene. Someone died yesterday!"

Unperturbed, Simon poured himself a coffee. "Did you know the dead man? Did I? No! Neither of us had anything to do with his death. If anything, we should be angry with him. His ill-timed death has thrown our production off schedule."

"Maybe we should cancel the film," Lance suggested.

Jaspar gave him a sharp look of disapproval.

Simon reared back in outrage. "Cancel it? You must be joking. It's out of the question. That ship has sailed. Or in our case, didn't sail…" He laughed at his own joke. "Principal photography starts Monday."

"I agree. There's no turning back," Jaspar said with a quick nod.

Lance's expression showed that he wasn't convinced.

Simon put his hand on Lance's shoulder. "This is no time for naysayers." Simon waved the script in the air. "I'm going to take this sow's ear and turn it into a silk purse."

"Sorry, Simon. I'm not thinking straight. I didn't sleep," Lance said.

Simon eyed Lance and shook his head. "It looks like it. Go home, take a shower and change your clothes." He pointed at Lance's coffee cup. "First, finish your coffee and have something to eat."

Simon took a croissant and turned to Ava. "And you are?"

"Sorry. I should have introduced her. This is Ava Sext," Jaspar replied. "She's going to be working with us."

"What happened to your assistant in London?" Simon asked. He grinned. "Don't tell me. I can guess. The infamous Martin Scotsdale has struck again."

"You hit the nail on the head. Did you pass by the set this morning?" Jaspar asked Simon.

"Not yet. Nate texted me. He's there with Claire, the assistant director. Decoration, costumes, makeup and lighting will be arriving at ten. Losing the barge was a blow," Simon admitted. "We're not ready for the roof scene, but we'll make it. I have some great ideas."

"Is the set the next garden over?" Ava asked.

Simon nodded. "Yes. The fact that it's next door simplifies things for the production."

"My aunt says we can use the roof platform to shoot," Lance told Simon. "It will be great for the establishing shot."

"I already told you that I'm not interested. That's your vision of the film. I'm the director. I have my own ideas. Stick to producing, Lance," Simon said sharply.

Lance was crest-fallen.

Simon raised his eyebrows and looked around the production office. "Where's the actor? He was supposed to be here at 9:45," Simon said to Jaspar.

"My watch says 9:44, so I'm right on time," a deep male voice boomed.

Ava looked up. Henri was striding toward them. He was dressed in a pale blue shirt, jeans and immaculate white sneakers. His salt and pepper hair curled around his face.

Immediately, Simon strode over to Henri. Circling, Simon examined him from head to foot. "The resemblance is remarkable. He's the same height as Ian and the same weight. His facial profile is a perfect match. If I had to, I could even do close-ups!" Simon exclaimed, delighted. He turned to Jaspar. "Where did you find him?"

Ignoring Simon's rude behavior, Henri smiled. "I believe introductions are in order. I'm Henri DeAth. You are?"

"Simon Hepplewhite, the director," Simon replied with a slight bow.

Suddenly, Lance sprang to life. "I'm Lance LeGris, the French producer. This is Ava Sext. She works in production. We're happy you're here."

Henri smiled at Lance and Ava. "Pleased to meet you."

Ava smiled back at Henri. Lance's introduction showed that he didn't know that she knew Henri. She eyed Jaspar who confirmed what she was thinking with a quick, almost imperceptible nod of his head.

Henri turned to Simon. "To answer your other question, Jaspar found me on the quay down the street. He bought a book from me. I run a bookstand on the Quai Malaquais."

Simon pursed his lips. "I apologize. I can be a real ass at times."

Jaspar let out a peal of laughter. "At times?"

The laughter burst the tension that had been building between Simon and the others.

"Touché," Simon said, amused. "Bravo, Jaspar. You have an eye. Without Henri, we would have been hard-pressed to shoot the roof scene." He turned to Henri. "You have a strong personality. That's good. It will transfer onto the screen. Have you ever acted?"

"Until now, no," Henri replied.

"The first time is a bit nerve-wracking. And then there's the waiting…" Simon explained.

Henri looked puzzled.

"Lots of waiting," Lance added with a knowing look. "When people see a film, they imagine that the director turned on the camera, said "action" and filmed the entire scene from start to finish. In reality, any scene is made up of lots of shots taken at different distances and angles. Each shot means moving the lighting and the camera. Break down and set up can take forever. For actors, that means waiting."

"Not to mention that the scenes in films aren't shot in order, so you might die the first day on the set," Jaspar said.

There was a stricken silence.

"I intend to stay alive... At least, until the end of my scene," Henri said with a smile.

"Your scene is an action scene. You'll be running across the roof," Simon explained.

"Those two minutes of film will take two entire nights if we get it right or longer if we don't. It's a complex shot," Jaspar warned.

"I'm ready to try," Henri responded with a warm smile.

Simon smiled at Henri. "That's the spirit. Let's get you to wardrobe and makeup." He turned to the others. "We'll be on the set if you need us."

Jaspar's phone beeped. It was a text message. As he read it, a cloud passed over his face.

"Anything serious?" Simon asked as he stared at Jaspar.

Jaspar looked up from his phone and sighed in exasperation. "The usual production snafus. Nothing to worry about."

Simon finished his coffee and tossed the paper cup in the garbage. "Ready, Henri?"

The two men walked off chatting as if they were long lost friends. Watching the men leave, Ava was in awe of Henri's ability to win over even the most hostile person. It was a talent she wished she had.

As the men neared the door, Nate entered.

"Simon! Catch!" Nate shouted.

Startled, Simon looked up. Nate tossed him a set of keys. Simon caught them and stared at them with a puzzled look in his face.

"Claire found them on the quay. You must have dropped them yesterday," Nate said.

"Thanks!" Simon replied as his ears turned bright red. He stuffed the keys in his pocket and left with Henri.

Nate joined Lance, Jaspar and Ava. Seeing the expression on Jaspar's face, Nate froze. "What's wrong?"

"The good or the bad?" Jaspar asked.

Hearing that, Lance went white.

Nate crossed his arm, combative. "Start with the good…"

"The good? Martin is in Paris," Jason said.

Lance looked puzzled. "His Eurostar isn't due in till this afternoon."

"He got here early," Jaspar said.

"Where is he?" Nate asked, all business.

Jaspar sighed. "At the apartment we rented for him. The building's *concierge* called my assistant in London to complain that he had smoked a pipe in the elevator."

"What's the bad?" Ava asked in a low voice.

"Someone has to go get him," Jaspar said.

Ava looked from left to right. All three men were staring at her.

"He's much nicer to women than men," Jaspar said.

"On a scale of one to ten, how much nicer?" Ava asked, narrowing her eyes.

Jaspar was silent.

"If he's too much for you, call me," Nate said. "I'll come to the rescue."

"No, thank you. I can do it," Ava said, irritated by Nate's condescending offer.

"From my experience of working with Ava, Martin is the one who will be calling us to be rescued," Jaspar replied with a grin.

Pleased by the compliment, Ava held her head high.

"I have bad news, too," Nate said.

"What is it?" Lance asked.

"Rain is forecast for Tuesday and Wednesday night," Nate said.

"We start shooting on Sunday?" Lance asked.

"I don't see any other option," Nate replied.

Jaspar pointed to the office. "Let's look at the planning and see what needs to be done."

"The codes and keys to Martin's place are in the office," Lance said to Ava.

Everyone headed to a glassed-in office at the back of the production office.

"This is where we hide out when things get too dicey," Jaspar joked.

Lance walked over to a desk that was covered with papers scattered every which way. "I'm not known for my neatness," he said with an apologetic smile as he began to hunt through the mess.

"The apartment we rented for Martin isn't far from here. You can be there in minutes," Jaspar told Ava.

Lance pulled a large envelope from the desk and waved it in the air, triumphant. "*Et voilà!*" He handed it to Ava. "The address and a map are inside along with the code and a double of the keys. There are two codes. One is for the entrance to the garden. The second is for the building."

Suddenly, Nate's face clouded over. He stormed past everyone toward the bulletin board on the far wall and ripped a piece of paper off it. "What the hell is this?" He held the paper up for everyone to see.

YOU KNOW WHO DID IT! was written on it.

Lance paled. A look of horror ran across his face.

Jaspar tightened his jaw. "Is this someone's idea of a joke?"

Nate looked at the paper in his hand and crumpled it up. "If it is, it isn't funny. I suggest we keep this to ourselves. With all that's going on, we don't want to spook the production."

Ava eyed the three men. All three were troubled, very troubled. But then so was she.

CHAPTER 12

Ava's heart was beating so loudly, it was deafening. Each heartbeat echoed the words she had just read in the production office: You know who did it.

The three men had been shaken.

None of them had taken the note lightly…

Could one of them have killed the man on the barge?

Ava took a deep breath. She needed to rein in her imagination before it got away from her. There was nothing to prove that any of the men were involved in the man's death. On the other hand, there was nothing to prove that they weren't.

Uneasy, she walked at a snail's pace. To shake off the feeling of impending doom, she turned her attention to her surroundings.

The rue Saint-André-des-Arts, a narrow street dating from the 13th century, was one of Ava's favorite streets in Paris. On any other day, she would have popped into the herbal shop with its old fashioned wooden shelves lined with mysterious white bags of dried herbs. The herbalist would tell her which herbs cured insomnia or gout while mixing up a potion -- perhaps a love potion -- for another client. Ava would have then wandered up the street to a tiny hole-in-the-wall jewelry shop where you could find anything from handmade Mexican silver bangle bracelets to rings with brightly colored Brazilian stones. Another favorite shop was the gadget store where you could buy banana slicers, heated ice cream scoopers, or even a carrot sharpener, not that Ava's carrots needed sharpening. However, today her mind was elsewhere.

Ava didn't need her sleuthing sixth sense to tell her that something was seriously out of kink on the film *Death on the Quai*.

One could argue that a death on a quay in a film called *Death on the Quai* was a coincidence. After all, Loulou worked with Jaspar, and her arrival at Ava's door really had been a coincidence. But the paper pinned to the board that had so shocked Lance, Nate and Jaspar was not a coincidence. Someone had written it and had pinned it to the board.

Could Nate, Lance, or Jaspar have known the man on the barge?

Ava wasn't entirely convinced that the man's death was murder. It might have been an accident. However, she was convinced that the dead man was linked to the note in the production office. Whoever had pinned the paper up had done it for a reason. The note might have been intended to smoke the guilty party out. Or it might be a warning. It was too early to say.

Ava tried to imagine Lance in the role of murderer. Try as she might, she just couldn't envision it. It seemed impossible.

However, in her short career as a sleuth, Ava had said impossible before and had been wrong. Murderers didn't always look like murderers. In fact, they rarely did.

But in this case, Ava was sure that Lance had not killed the man. Lance was a bungler. If he had been involved in the death, he probably would have fallen in the Seine afterward or done something equally as obvious to draw attention to his guilt.

Could Jaspar or Nate be involved in the death?

Ava ruled Jaspar out immediately for personal reasons. Plus, he had hired her. Why hire a sleuth if you're the guilty party?

Could Nate have killed the man? He was the one who had found the body, and he'd kept the others off the barge. Maybe he had known what he would discover when he went to the barge yesterday afternoon. On the other hand, Nate was very efficient. If he had wanted to kill the man, he would have found a spot to do it that wasn't linked to the film.

Ava stopped in mid-step as yet another idea popped into her head... Perhaps the killer had written the note so the men would suspect each other when in reality the killer was none of the three.

Reluctantly, Ava turned her attention to her present situation. She was the sacrificial victim the production was sending into the ogre's lair. She would survive Martin Scotsdale, but she wasn't looking forward to the experience. She had little patience for unpleasant people, and she had a case to solve. On the other hand, Martin might have some insight into what was going on. She wondered if he knew about the dead man.

In a bid to postpone the inevitable confrontation, Ava headed to a quaint café further down the street. What was required in a situation like this was another quick jolt of caffeine. It would give her the needed energy to deal with the infamous screenwriter and more time to mull over what was going on. She might even order a *chausson aux pommes*, an apple turnover.

As she crossed the street to the café, a black sedan drove past her and pulled over a few feet up the street.

A woman slid out of the sedan's back seat.

Ava frowned. The woman looked familiar. Incredibly elegant in wide trousers and a pink Chanel jacket with the glass pendant around her neck, the woman wore large black sunglasses and had a floppy pink straw hat on her head.

It was Madame LeGris.

Ava blinked and looked at the woman again to make sure she

wasn't seeing things.

She wasn't...

It was Madame LeGris.

Madame LeGris walked up to a building, entered the code and vanished inside as the sedan pulled away.

Stunned, Ava stared at the building.

What she had just witnessed was a coincidence.

Another coincidence.

She was being snowed over by coincidences, and she didn't like it. If this kept up, she'd be swept away by an avalanche of coincidences.

Ducking into the café, Ava sat down at a window table and peered out at the building across the way. This time, there was no stopping her imagination. It immediately went into overdrive.

Question One: Why had Madame LeGris gone there?

Ava went for a very Parisian solution. Madame LeGris had a lover. Her husband was dead. There was nothing wrong with having a lover. In addition, age was no obstacle to *affairs of the heart* as they were called in France.

Not completely satisfied with that solution, Ava ran over other reasons Madame LeGris might have entered the building. She could be consulting a clairvoyant or having a session with a chiropractor. Finally, Ava settled on a more mundane and much less tantalizing explanation... Madame LeGris was visiting a friend.

A waiter appeared. "What can I get you?"

"Nothing today," Ava said with a cheerful smile as she stood up and left.

Anxious to find out more about the mysterious Madame LeGris, she crossed the street and walked up to the building's door. She pushed it, but it was locked. Without the code, there was no way she could get inside.

She lingered outside for a few minutes. Just as she was about to give up and head to Martin's place, a chic blond-haired middle-aged woman wearing jeans, a long-sleeved T-shirt and mirrored sunglasses came out of the building.

Ava watched the woman walk off, counted to three and sprinted to the door. She blocked it with her foot seconds before it slammed shut.

The woman was a stroke of luck! A sign that the heavens looked favorably at Ava's sleuthing.

Ava slipped into the building and stood in the entrance hallway. There was nothing special about it. It resembled entrance hallways in many old Parisian buildings.

Striding over to the mailboxes on the wall, Ava ran her eyes over the names written on each box. There were the usual French names and a few foreign-sounding ones. None of them rang a bell. She took out her phone and snapped photos of the names. Knowing who lived in the building might come in handy later.

Content, Ava exited the building and lingered on the corner for a few more minutes on the off chance that Madame LeGris would appear. When she didn't, Ava began to walk.

Destination -- Martin Scotsdale's apartment.

Ava strolled down the rue de l'Eperon and turned onto the rue de Jardinet, a street that dead-ended in the cobblestoned Cour de Rohan, a series of three private courtyards built in the 1500s. The moment you set foot inside the courtyards, you were in a different Paris.

Hidden behind the Cour de Rohan's tall gates were remnants of the original medieval wall that once encircled Paris. There were also buildings dating from the Renaissance. One of the courtyards had huge terracotta planters filled with flowering plants like you'd find in a village in Provence in southeastern France.

Ava punched in the code and went into the first courtyard. She was immediately overwhelmed by the odor of roses and honeysuckle. She closed her eyes and took a deep breath as the first notes of a Bach cantata began to echo through the courtyard. She opened her eyes, stepped back and eyed the top floor of the building where Martin's apartment was situated. Its windows were wide open. The Bach cantata was coming from there. Ava was reassured. Music soothed the wild beast or so it was said.

Taking her courage in hand, she entered the building.

The building's interior walls tilted slightly forward, the way walls in very old French buildings did. Ava decided to take the stairs up to the top. It would give her a few more minutes to put off the inevitable. From what Lance, Nate and Jaspar had told her, she was worried that she'd have to drag Martin to the set by force.

Walking slowly, she wound her way up to the top floor. She gripped the banister firmly to keep her balance. Slowing at an open window, she watched birds flitting in and out of a tall tree outside. Their chirping made her forget everything that was going on for a few brief instants before a glance at Martin's window made it all come crashing back.

With a heavy sigh, she continued to the top floor, stopping in front of the only door on the landing. "Out-of-order" was taped over its doorbell. Taking a deep breath, she knocked three times and stood tall, ready for anything.

The door swung open instantly. A tall man in his late fifties with wavy brown hair, wearing bright yellow trousers, a pink checked shirt and white socks with sandals was standing in front of her. The man's face was long and thin. He had a three-day beard and was wearing glasses with bright pink plastic frames. He stared at her, frowning.

"Can I help you?" the man asked, puzzled.

Ava smiled her biggest smile. "I'm Ava Sext. The production company sent me."

The man looked her over from head to foot. Without a word, he spun around, walked back into the apartment and settled into a French Bergère chair done up in pale yellow silk. He waved Ava in as Bach continued to play. "Come in. Don't be shy."

Ava stepped into the apartment. It was a loft apartment with exposed beams, whitewashed walls and elegant French furniture. Engravings of Parisian monuments hung on its walls.

The man's eyes were now closed. He moved his head to the music. When the cantata ended, he opened them and crooked his head to the side. "Ava Sext? I knew an Alistair Sext from Tunbridge Wells. Is he a relative?"

"Not that I know of," Ava said. Wary, she took stock of Martin Scotsdale. So far, he didn't appear to be the monster everyone had warned her about.

"You're probably lucky. I never liked Alistair. He was a fool, and I don't tolerate fools," Martin said with a sigh. "Where's Jaspar? I expected him to be at my door at the crack of dawn to drag me to the set."

"He thought you were arriving later today," Ava said.

Martin frowned. "Didn't I send him a text message that I was arriving early? I must have forgotten."

"When did you get here?" Ava asked.

Ignoring her question, Martin leapt to his feet. "What does it matter? I'm here now." He grabbed a pipe and matches off a marble-topped table and strode to an open window. He lit the pipe and leaned out. "I promised the owner that I wouldn't smoke inside. This is my compromise," he said with a mischievous smile.

Ava eyed the apartment again. It was full of light. The delicate furniture and Bach made it a haven of peace. Martin was the only discordant element in it.

Martin drew on his pipe and turned to Ava. "I lived here thirty years ago. A friend bought it years later and did it up. When I knew I was coming to Paris, I asked him if it was empty. It was. I had the production rent it." He eyed the apartment. "It didn't look like this back then. It was a dump. There was no heat, and the bathtub was in the kitchen. Still, I loved it."

Uneasy, Ava didn't like this new coincidence.

"I'm Martin Scotsdale, if you haven't guessed. They probably warned you about me. I can be cranky at my best."

"Jaspar did say that you were temperamental, but writers are known for their quirks," Ava said, before rushing to the heart of the matter. "I read your script. I can't wait to read the end."

Holding his pipe out the window, Martin winced. "Writers are also very good at seeing through people. You want to know if I finished the script?"

"Yes," Ava said, embarrassed at being caught out.

Martin shook his head in disapproval. "Civilization is going down the tubes because people don't take time to talk. In my opinion, small talk is anything but small. It's part of the very fabric of life. Did you know that at the turn of the century they used to assign conversation topics at dinners parties? I find that marvelous. People should talk about ideas. It would stop us from blathering on about ourselves. You're from London?"

"Yes," Ava responded.

"We Londoners recognize each other. I was born and bred in Mayfair. I still have a pied-à-terre there, but most of the time I live in Scotland."

Silent, Ava took this in. Being born in Mayfair explained a lot about Martin's sense of entitlement. Mayfair was a wealthy part of London. It had always been a wealthy part of London. It was near Harrods and Hyde Park. Somehow, Ava couldn't imagine Martin wandering the streets of Mayfair in his socks and sandals. But then wealthy Londoners were often eccentric, which was a nice way of saying they were odd.

"How did you get involved in this awful film?" Martin asked as he drew on his pipe.

"I've known Jaspar for years. We worked together once. As I was living in Paris, he asked me to join the production."

Martin exhaled. White smoke rose in the air and encircled his head. "Jaspar is a nice chap. You know how people say, "it's not you, it's me"? In my case, it's true. I don't like people telling me what to do. Having to write the script was pure torture. Have you read the book?"

"I skimmed through it," Ava replied.

Martin shook his head. "Believe me, that was more than enough. You don't want to waste your time. My script is much better. You'll see when I'm done."

Ava's heart sank. Martin hadn't finished the script.

Noticing the expression on her face, he laughed. "Don't worry. I wrote the ending. It needs a few final tweaks before the production reads it. Jaspar will have it tomorrow." Suddenly, an impish smile appeared on his face. "You read the script, how would you end it?"

"I'm not a writer," Ava protested.

Martin frowned. "You're intelligent. You have spirit. Surely, you can conjure up an ending!"

Ava hesitated. "I can see two endings."

Focused on what she was saying, Martin waited.

"The first ending is tragic. George turns everyone into the police as he is angry about the relationship between Ella and Matt."

Martin guffawed. "There's little chance of that happening!"

Ava fell silent. Watching Martin, she didn't doubt that he would be a worthy foe to anyone who stepped into his crosshairs.

"What's your second ending?" Martin asked.

"Ella takes the jewels and leaves the two men to sort it out," Ava replied.

Martin raised his eyebrows and frowned in disapproval. "She abandons the men she loves?"

"Yes. She decided to live life on her own terms. The men were holding her back." Ava was astonished by her own words. It was a complete reversal of her earlier thoughts on the script. Somehow, overnight, Ella had become a true free spirit, beholden to no one other than herself.

"My Ella wouldn't do that," Martin protested. "In my version, life goes on for all the protagonists, just not the way they thought it would. Ken would be surprised at how it ends."

"Ken?" Ava asked.

"I meant George," Martin said without missing a beat.

Ava raised her eyebrows. "So they don't die in the barge explosion? When I read the book, I thought they did."

"The book is complete and utter nonsense. The person who wrote it didn't understand the story. The book is a stripped-down look at a jewel heist. The writer dramatized the event without showing the slightest insight into the vagaries of the human heart. The characters don't exist. Who is Ken? Who is Matt? At times, the book does have a certain loud charm, like a bull in a china shop. If sappy, melodramatic plot contrivances move you, you'll like the book. Believe me, I had my work cut out for me."

Ava frowned. It was the second time Martin had said Ken.

Martin stamped his pipe out. "Enough of *Death on the Quai*. I need lunch and a beer."

"It's early for lunch," Ava protested. "Besides, I'm sure Jaspar, Lance and Simon are intending to have lunch with you."

Ignoring her protests, Martin nodded in agreement with himself. "There's a bistro on the rue de Buci that serves food all day. Give me five minutes." He disappeared into a room, closing the door behind him.

So much for my controlling the situation, Ava thought. Martin would go to the set when he wanted to and not a minute sooner. The best she could do was try and speed that up. One hour more or less wouldn't change anything.

However, it would give her time to talk to Martin without the others. She imagined the meeting between Simon and the screenwriter wouldn't be smooth sailing.

Taking advantage of Martin's absence, Ava strolled around the apartment. She peered into the modern kitchen, which was sleek and outfitted with the latest appliances. She had a hard time imagining a tub in the center of it.

Hearing Martin return, she went back to the living room.

Martin grabbed his pipe. "Lunch?"

"Lunch," Ava replied with a nod of her head.

CHAPTER 13

Despite the early hour, the café was packed with people eating *steak-frites* -- steak and French fries -- the café's specialty. When Martin and Ava arrived, the head waiter greeted Martin like a long lost friend, and led them to a prime table on the outdoor terrace. From there, they could watch life on the picturesque rue de Buci.

The street was in the Saint-Germain-des-Prés neighborhood. It was home to an outdoor food market, flower shops, book stores and several cafés with outdoor terraces. As the cafés were popular tourist haunts, their menus were written in English, German, Spanish and Italian.

Martin settled into his seat and waved the waiter over. "A cold beer for me and a *croque monsieur*." Martin turned to Ava. "What would you like?"

Ava thought for an instant. A croque monsieur was a grilled ham and cheese sandwich. A *croque madame* was a grilled ham and cheese sandwich with a fried egg on top of it. It seemed like a good compromise between a late breakfast and an early lunch. "I'll have a croque madame and sparkling mineral water with a twist of lemon."

The waiter nodded and left.

"I'm curious to see the set," Martin said. "Nate sent me photos of the barge. It's perfect."

Ava caught her breath. Martin didn't know about the change in the shooting schedule. That meant he didn't know about the dead man. After weighing her options, she decided that she wasn't going to be the bearer of bad news.

Martin leaned back in his chair. "The boat was the one successful scene in the book. It has everything -- a beautiful location, an explosion and it ends with a mystery... What will happen next? Are they dead? Is the jewel lost forever? Will love triumph? And if so, how?"

The waiter brought their drinks and set them on the table.

Martin took a sip of his beer, content. "What more could I ask for? A cold beer, beautiful weather, Paris and a charming lunch companion... Not to mention a film."

Ava squeezed the lemon into her mineral water and let Martin talk, something he didn't need any encouragement to do.

"Given the budget, I imagine the explosion will be a rudimentary puff of smoke, some stock shots of an explosion and then "Fade to Black". Smoke and mirrors! However, even a fake explosion will add some desperately needed production value to the film," Martin explained. Suddenly, a serious look spread across his face. He put his beer down and peered into Ava's eyes. "There is something I don't understand."

"What's that?" Ava asked, hoping he was about to reveal a clue that would help her discover what was going on.

"Why in God's name is Jaspar working with Lance? I spoke with Lance on the phone. He was terrified of me," Martin said with a chuckle. He shook his head in disapproval. "You need to be tough to make a film."

Ava was silent. Martin's words meant that he wasn't aware of the contract's stipulations. Seeing that he was waiting for an answer, Ava rolled her eyes. "Lance lets Jaspar run the show. Jaspar has a partner, but one he controls."

"That makes sense," Martin said with a quick nod. "Better the devil you can control than the angel you can't…"

Ava wondered if Martin was the devil that the film's backer hoped to control.

"However, your theory doesn't explain Simon Heppleworth.

He's an ass," Martin said.

"You've met Simon?" Ava asked. *Hadn't Jaspar said that the two men had never met?*

Martin nodded. "Ages ago. To be charitable, he was an incompetent ass back then. I can't imagine that he's changed."

"When did you meet him?" Ava asked in as neutral a tone as possible.

Before Martin could answer, the waiter brought over their sandwiches.

Immediately, Martin cut a piece off his croque monsieur and bit into it. "Heaven." He eyed Ava. "I existed on these when I lived in Paris. I never tired of them. I intend to eat one a day for the rest of my stay. Save the foie gras and champagne for someone else. A cold beer and a croque monsieur at a sidewalk café in my old neighborhood... What more could I ask for?" He eyed the people walking by. "I should have come back here earlier," he said in a voice tinged with nostalgia.

"Were you a student in Paris?" Ava asked as she sprinkled pepper on the egg that topped her sandwich.

Martin shook his head. "No. I was a struggling writer in a garret."

"With a bathtub in the kitchen," Ava added with a smile.

Martin took a large sip of his beer. "It was back then that I met Simon. He worked on my film."

Ava almost choked. "You worked on a film in Paris?"

Martin nodded. "My first script was shot in Paris. It was a no-budget production with non-professional actors and an inexperienced crew. Simon was the AD, the assistant director."

Ava was stunned. What Martin was telling her changed her take on everything. If she had any remaining doubts, they were gone. *What was happening wasn't a coincidence, it was planned.*

Martin raised his beer in the air. "To first films."

Ava raised her glass of water.

Martin stopped her. "Toasting with water is unlucky." He waved the waiter over. "A glass of wine for the lady." He turned to Ava. "Red, white?"

Ava eyed her croque madame. "White."

"Sancerre?" the waiter asked.

"Sancerre," Ava said. Sancerre, made from Sauvignon Blanc grapes from the Loire Valley, would go well with her sandwich.

"Make that two glasses," Martin said to the departing waiter.

"Was the film distributed?" Ava asked as she took a bite of her sandwich. It was wonderful. The pepper and the egg were perfect together.

Martin's expression clouded over. "It was never completed. The producer/director ran off with the money. Devastated, I moved back to London and began to work there. I haven't been to Paris since."

"But it's right across the channel," Ava exclaimed, bewildered.

"The distance was psychological. I lost my dream when the film shut down. A first film is like a first love," Martin said with a sad expression on his face.

"Why didn't you become a director?" Ava asked. "In my experience, screenwriters want to become directors. Directors want to become producers…"

"And producers want to become God. While God wants to be an actor," Martin joked.

"What was the film about?" Ava asked. "A jewel heist?"

Martin was aghast. "Heavens, no! It was a love story. Boy meets girl. Boy falls in love with girl. Girl falls in love with someone else. Admittedly, it was not very original. Although I thought it was at the time."

The waiter brought them their wine.

Martin gripped his glass and raised it in the air. "To film!"

Ava raised her glass in the air. "To *Death on the Quai!*"

"My version," Martin added with a wicked grin.

They both took a sip of their wine.

"This is very refreshing," Martin said in approval. "I might even add a glass of Sancerre to my daily routine."

"Where was your film shot?" Ava asked.

"In this neighborhood, not far from here. It was in a *hôtel particulier* that belonged to a countess. The director who was also the producer was an opportunistic cad who flattered her into letting us shoot there."

It couldn't be the same hôtel particulier, Ava thought, although she knew it was.

Martin snorted. "He was so shameless that he even finagled the countess into financing part of the film. I shouldn't complain. I should thank him. The ten days of shooting before the film shut down were the happiest days of my life."

"How did your story end?" Ava asked.

"Tragically. The young woman killed herself. When the first man realized that he couldn't live without her, it was too late. She was dead."

"And the other man?" Ava asked.

"He vanished." Martin shook his head and took another bite of his croque monsieur sandwich. "It was complete blather. I was young. You don't kill yourself or someone else for love," Martin said. "Murder is a serious business."

Ava raised her eyebrows.

Seeing her reaction, Martin laughed. "I'm speaking as a screenwriter. I've killed off numerous characters over the years. I always feel bad. Even if they are villainous, you start to like them. But I've become ruthless. When it's time for someone to die, they die. No holding back." Martin downed his wine.

Ava's cell phone rang. She answered. Ava spoke loudly for Martin's benefit. "Jaspar! Yes. Everything is fine. I've just finished having a quick bite with Martin. We'll be right there."

Martin grabbed the phone from her. "Jaspar, don't worry. The script is done." He listened for an instant and burst out laughing. He ended the call and handed the phone to Ava.

"What is it?" Ava asked Martin.

"Jaspar told me that if I needed rescuing from you to let him know," Martin said with a guffaw.

CHAPTER 14

In good spirits after lunch, Martin strolled down the rue de Buci with Ava in the direction of the production office. He walked at a leisurely pace, eying the panorama of Parisian life unfolding around him with endless delight.

"I should have come back sooner. I was a fool. Paris is magical!" Martin proclaimed to no one in particular.

Troubled, Ava didn't respond. With each step, she was edging closer to the moment of truth. Sooner or later, she would have to tell Martin that the shoot on the barge had been postponed because of a dead man, and that the film was being shot at the same mansion where his first film had been filmed. Ava wondered what his reaction to those revelations would be. She suspected that they would resurrect the irascible Martin who had so far been absent.

When they reached the rue Saint-André-des-Arts, Ava opted for sooner. Taking a deep breath, she began to speak. "Martin, there was a change in the production schedule."

Immediately on his guard, he slowed and stared at her. "What change?"

"There was some problem with the barge. They've decided to start the shoot with another scene," Ava said. Coward that she was, she avoided the issue of the dead man entirely.

Martin's eyes drilled into her. "What scene is that?"

"The rooftop escape scene," Ava responded.

Martin was silent. "Where are they shooting it?"

"At a mansion just down the street," Ava said, her voice trailing off.

Martin's face clouded over. "Of course, where else?" he murmured. The expression on his face became cold and distant. Without a word, he walked off. He didn't need her to tell him where the set was.

Worried, Ava followed him. Watching him walk, she sensed he was preparing himself for the worse. She, too, was preparing herself for the worst.

When they reached the street the mansion was located on,

Martin stopped and stared down the street with a dazed expression on his face. "The street hasn't changed at all. It's like time's stood still."

Tightening his jaw, he started off toward the mansion. To Ava's surprise, he walked past it and halted in front of a tiny triangular-shaped shop that occupied the space between one of the mansion's exterior walls and the wall of an adjoining building. The shop looked as if it had been closed for a long time. Its front window was streaked with dirt. Posters for old cultural events were pasted over it.

"This used to be our bar. It was so small you couldn't fit more than six people inside," Martin said with a nostalgic smile as he rubbed his palm over the dirty window in an attempt to see the interior.

The only thing visible was a faded red velvet curtain that crossed the front of the shop.

Staring at the red curtain, Martin's expression darkened. "But those days are over." Whirling around, he strode back to the mansion's open coach doors and stepped through them.

Worried, Ava dogged his steps.

A few crew members were milling around a snack table under a tent in the courtyard in front of the mansion. Ava recognized one of them as Claire, the assistant director. There was no sign of Lance, Jaspar, Nate or Henri.

Ava eyed the mansion. Like the LeGris mansion, it was perfectly maintained. However, it was larger and more imposing than the LeGris mansion. The stones in the courtyard had been sandblasted until they were whiter than white. Wild rose bushes climbed up the mansion's walls. Olive trees in wooden planters were placed in rows around the courtyard.

Without a word, Martin headed straight to the mansion's front door and pushed it open. Unsure of what to do, Ava followed him.

The vast entrance hall resembled that of the LeGris mansion. The two buildings were built along the same lines. Like in the LeGris mansion, an imposing stone staircase to their right led to the upper floors. An enormous Venetian chandelier made of Murano glass in bright jewel tones hung down from the ceiling. While the mansion was just as luxurious as the LeGris mansion, a feeling of sadness lingered over it.

Martin spun around slowly and looked at everything as if it were the first time. He didn't speak. He was so pale that Ava feared he would faint.

Suddenly, he bounded toward the stairs. Grabbing the black and gold wrought-iron banister, he took the stairs two at a time. At the landing, he slowed. Then he strode over to a pair of gold-edged mirrored doors, pushed them open with both hands, and stood there gazing in.

The doors gave onto a large reception hall. The hall's walls were mirrored. Two enormous Venetian chandeliers made of Murano glass in tones of red, green and yellow hung from the ceiling. An intricate parquet floor shone in the sunlight streaming through the open windows, while colored reflections from the chandeliers danced across it.

A dark-haired man was standing at the far end of the room with his back to the door. His arms were outstretched like a scarecrow. A wardrobe woman circled him, pinning his clothing. Another woman was styling the man's slicked-back dark hair.

Turning, the wardrobe woman frowned when she saw Martin and Ava. "You can't come in here!"

Martin ignored the woman and strode to the center of the room. He spun around and broke out in laughter. "I was terrified of coming back here. It's just a room."

The dark-haired man put his arms down. "I was hoping for a break. My arms were going to sleep."

Hearing the man's voice, Ava stared in disbelief.

The man was Henri.

But it was a Henri she had never seen before. It was a Henri who looked exactly like Ian Granger. Henri had a small mustache, slicked-back dark hair and had thick horn-rimmed glasses perched on his nose. He was unrecognizable.

"Ian Granger?" Martin asked, stepping toward him.

Henri shook his head. "Henri DeAth," he said was a slight bow of his head.

Hearing the pronunciation of Henri's last name, a deep furrow appeared on Martin's forehead. "Death?"

Henri nodded. "It's an old Flemish name. Its pronunciation often surprises English speakers."

Martin snapped out of his trancelike state. "I went to school with a Henri Pigg. Growing up with a name like that must have been torture for him. Moreover, he blushed easily. Poor pink-faced Piggy." Martin shook his head at the memory of his classmate and held his hand out to Henri. "I'm Martin Scotsdale."

The men shook hands.

Hearing Martin's name, the wardrobe woman and the hairstylist eyed one another alarmed. Clearly, Martin's reputation had preceded him.

Ava stood at the entrance to the room unable to get over Henri's transformation. She examined him from head to foot. "I didn't recognize you."

"That's the magic of cinema," Henri joked. With a warm smile, he turned to Martin. "Why were you afraid of coming back here?"

"It's a long story. I made a film in this very room years ago… thirty years ago to be exact. In my mind, the set remained untouched. Nothing had changed. But of course, things have changed. The countess isn't here. The crew I worked with is long gone," Martin said. He smiled at the two women. "And as charming as these two ladies are, they weren't even born then."

Eyeing each other, the two women took this as an opportunity to leave.

The wardrobe woman stepped toward Henri. "You can change back into your own clothes. If anyone is looking for us, we'll be at the snack tent. Do you want us to bring you anything?"

Henri shook his head. "We'll be down soon."

The hairstylist pointed at Henri's mustache. "I'll take that off once Simon has seen you."

The women hurried out of the room without a backward glance.

Henri removed his glasses and strolled over to the window. He gazed down at the vast garden "What a coincidence that the production is using the same set."

Simon shook his head. "It's not a coincidence. It's deliberate."

Henri raised his eyebrows. "Deliberate? Why do you say that?"

Martin shrugged. "I have no idea. I've asked myself that ever since I started adapting the book. Why did the production choose me? My days in the sun are long gone. For a brief instant, I was arrogant enough to believe it was my talent. When I heard that I'd be working with Simon Heppleworth, I knew something was wrong. I continued anyway."

Ava could see that Henri had a lot of questions. However, he let Martin speak.

"Whatever they're looking for it's too late. The past is over. If I didn't have the answer then, I won't have it now," Martin said.

Ava was about to burst. *Who was this mysterious "they" he referred to? What answer? What was the question?*

Martin fell silent and stared at Henri. He narrowed his eyes. "Do I know you from somewhere? You seem familiar."

"It's possible. I work on the Quai Malaquais. I'm a bookseller when I'm not masquerading as Ian Granger," Henri said gesturing toward his hair and mustache.

"That must be it. I was on the quay yesterday," Martin said. "Where is Simon? I wonder if he's changed after all these years?"

"He's probably downstairs. Give me a second to put on my own clothing, and we'll go look for him," Henri said as he slipped behind a curtain in the corner and pulled it closed.

Martin walked to the window and gazed out with a wistful expression on his face. "This is where she killed herself."

"Who?" Ava asked, breathless.

"The character in my film. I should have let her live. I was wrong," Martin said with regret.

Minutes later, Henri pulled the curtain open. He was dressed in his own clothing. The thick horn-rimmed glasses were in his pocket, but his hair was still dark and the mustache was still there.

Ava stared at his new hair color. Henri was a good-looking man, but he was drop-dead gorgeous with his dark hair. Missing the old Henri, Ava frowned. "Will your hair color last long?"

"After I wash it three or four times, I'll be my old self," Henri said as he ran his hand through his hair. "It's odd. I feel like I've gone back in time."

Martin nodded. "Time is playing tricks with everyone today." He paused. "Would you like a tour?"

"Of the set?" Henri asked.

"My set... I want to see what's changed," Martin said.

Before Henri could respond, Martin walked to the far end of the room and pushed open a door. Ava and Henri followed him through it.

They were in another room that was all gold and mirrors. It was much smaller than the reception hall. Angels were painted on the room's ceiling. Heavy gold drapes covered the windows.

"This was the countess's *boudoir*, her private sitting room. She would sit here in an elegant silk dressing gown and talk on the phone all morning while we filmed in the room next door."

"Were you the director?" Henri asked.

Martin burst out laughing. "Worse. I was the screenwriter. As it was my first film, I suffered. It was written with my blood and guts. When it ended, I died..."

"Was Ken the director?" Ava asked.

"How did you know that?" Martin asked with a sharp frown before he nodded, lost to his memories. "Ken Waters... He was the director and the producer. He made the film possible, and he killed it."

Martin walked to a door at the left of the sitting room and pushed it open. It gave onto a larger room with more gold gilt and mirrors. He strode over to a series of mirrored doors that lined a wall and flung them open, one by one. Empty clothing racks and shelves were inside. The faint odor of violets wafted from them. "The countess's couture dresses were here," he said pointing. "Her furs were there. She seemed to have a different fur for every occasion, and it was summer." He gestured to a safe at the back of the closet. "She kept her jewelry there. Nothing was too over the top for the countess. Diamonds for breakfast, rubies for lunch, and dinner was diamonds, rubies, pearls with a few opals and sapphires thrown in. She wasn't a snob. Far from it. She was at the age where she didn't care what people thought and rich enough to do what she wanted."

"Is that her coat of arms over the doorway downstairs?" Henri asked.

Martin nodded. "It's the Liccacio coat of arms. It's an old Italian family. Her family had two different popes in it. The Liccacios were the rich among the rich. She was the end of a line. I have nothing bad to say about the countess. She was a lovely woman. I almost felt sorry that she had fallen in with Ken."

"Ken Waters?" Henri asked.

"The very same," Martin said as he closed the closet doors. "Ken was a ladies' man, a charmer. He could charm the birds out of the trees. But give him his due, he was also creative and had vision. The countess saw herself as a patroness of the arts. She wanted to transcend the world she came from. In another century she would have been a patroness like the Medicis. Instead, she financed my film. Perhaps she saw it as a way to live other lives. Dressed in her furs and jewels, she'd come to cheap dives in the Latin Quarter with us and stay up until dawn, drinking and dancing."

"How did Ken kill the film?" Ava asked, anxious to get to the bottom of what was going on.

Martin hesitated. "He left with the money she'd given us. Maybe he saw the writing on the wall. She had a new protégé. I'd hoped he had enough sway over her that we'd finish the film. He did, but we didn't. She gave him more money, and he disappeared with it. After only ten days of shooting, it was all over."

Ava frowned. Something told her that Martin was not telling them the whole truth.

"Was it a heist film?" Henri asked.

Martin chuckled. "Do you know the story of the screenwriter who had writer's block?"

Henri shook his head no.

"In the middle of the night, the screenwriter has a revelation. He wakes up, reaches through the dark for a pen and paper and writes down his idea. He falls into a fitful sleep, convinced he has found that rare million-dollar idea," Martin said with a smile.

"And that is?" Henri asked, taking the bait.

"Boy meets girl," Martin said. "His idea was boy meets girl. That was my idea, too. Of course, my story was set in Paris. That makes any story better."

"Shall we get a coffee?" Henri asked.

Martin accepted with a nod.

Chatting, the men walked out of the room.

Ava followed them out. Henri's charm had worked again. Not that she had done badly at taming the wild beast. She had discovered the existence of Martin's film.

As they went down the stairs to the ground floor, Nate came running up toward them. The expression on his face showed that he had heard that the infamous Martin Scotsdale was on the premises.

The ever-frowning Nate forced himself to smile at Martin. "Martin, how good to see you."

Martin shook his head. "Nate, you don't like me. I don't like you. Let's not pretend otherwise. Where's Simon?"

"Simon Heppleworth?" Nate asked, worried. "He's here somewhere."

"And Jaspar and Lance?" Ava asked.

"They had to go to the production office," Nate said in an odd tone of voice.

Sensing something was wrong, Henri turned to Martin to deflect attention from Nate. "I don't know about you, but I'm ready for that coffee."

Martin eyed Nate with a suspicious frown and followed Henri and Ava down the stairs. Watching them, Nate pulled out his phone and made a call.

From the bottom of the staircase, Martin stared up at Nate. "Something seems to be wrong..."

"From my brief time here today, I've learned that something always goes wrong in film," Henri exclaimed.

"At least, he didn't ask me if I'd finished the script," Martin said with a roguish smile.

"He had me get that information," Ava confessed.

Martin turned to Ava. "If I were in his shoes, I'd have done the same thing. Beauty tames the beast, but that's another film."

Sitting in the shade of olive trees on the edge of the courtyard, Martin, Simon and Ava drank their coffees.

"Some things haven't changed," Martin said as he gazed around the courtyard. "These trees were here thirty years ago. They're over 100 years old. The countess had them brought from her estate in Tuscany."

"Martin hasn't been back in Paris since the film," Ava explained.

"Thirty years? That's a long time," Henri said, astonished. "How does it feel to be back?"

"Strange. Paris hasn't changed. I know I have. Although part of me feels the same until I look in the mirror," Martin admitted.

"But the voice in our head stays the same, doesn't it?" Henri asked.

Martin nodded. "And it always says the same thing despite my efforts to silence it." He leaned back in his chair. "So you're standing in for Ian in the roof scenes?"

"I'm not very keen about wandering across the roof," Henri said. "Although I prefer that to going through underground tunnels…"

Martin shook his head. "Tunnels would be too dark. The book had a rooftop scene and I stuck with it."

"The crew told me that the mansion is supposed to be haunted," Henri said.

Martin took out his pipe, lit it and then drew on it. "I don't believe in ghosts, but it's definitely haunted. Even the countess believed it was haunted."

Full of energy, Simon strode over toward them and eyed Henri. "If Ian Granger saw you in a mirror, he'd think you were him." He turned to Martin. "We haven't had the pleasure of meeting. Each time I was in London, you were in Scotland."

Martin stared at Simon with a frown. "Who are you?"

Simon was astonished. "Simon Heppleworth, the director."

Martin stood up and stared at Simon. "That's a lie. You're not Simon Heppleworth!"

"That would come as a surprise to my mother," Simon said as

his ears turned red. Suddenly, his eyes lit up in understanding. "You must have known my late cousin."

Martin frowned.

"He was also named Simon Heppleworth," Simon said.

"Late?" Martin asked, arching his eyebrows.

"He died in a trekking accident in Tibet twenty years ago. He worked in film in Paris for a while. He gave it up to become a vicar."

Martin opened his mouth to respond. Instead, he burst out laughing. "You fear the past, and it's not what you think." Suddenly, his expression darkened. "I wonder if the writer knows that you're the wrong Simon?"

Simon was amused. "As I have seen no proof that the writer even exists -- his book certainly isn't proof of that -- I don't know what he thinks. But if he does exist, maybe I'm the right Simon, and you're the wrong Martin."

A curious look spread across Martin's face. Something Simon had said alarmed him. "Maybe I am the wrong Martin." Martin turned to Ava. "You'll have the final pages tomorrow morning." White-faced, he walked off without a word.

Nate joined them. He stared at the departing Martin. "Where's he going? He just got here."

Simon let out a deep sigh and stared at Nate. "You and Jaspar warned me that Martin was difficult. You should have told me that he's mad as a hatter." He patted Henri on the shoulder. "Come with me. I want to explain your scene to you. You, too, Nate. I've changed some of my shots."

Ava watched the men walk off. Uneasy, she wondered what it would mean if Martin and Simon were both the right ones.

CHAPTER 15

Trying to wrap her mind around the fact that there were two Simon Heppleworths, Ava finished her coffee. It didn't seem plausible that there were two of them. It was the sort of plot device that you found in bad detective novels.

But this wasn't a novel.

This was real life, and there were two Simon Heppleworths. One of whom must be the right Simon Heppleworth and one who was the wrong Simon Heppleworth.

With a sigh, Ava stared at the mansion. There was no sign of Henri returning. She wanted to tell him what she had learned at lunch, but it would have to wait. It was time to go to the production office and find out more about the note, the mansion and the barge.

As she walked to the coach doors, she thought back to note on the board: *You know who did it.*

She had come up with more ideas about why someone might have written the note.

The first and most obvious was that the note's author did indeed know who had killed the man on the barge and was using the note to threaten the person. On the other hand, the note's author might not know who had killed the man and was using the note to smoke the guilty party out. A third possibility was that someone wanted to stop the production and was using the note to create chaos.

Ava had no idea who had written it so she had no idea what the person's motivation might have been. As for the three men's reactions… Jaspar and Lance had been shocked when they saw the note, while Nate had been annoyed and angry.

As she exited through the open coach doors, one last thought struck Ava… The note might have been written by one of the three men.

Stepping into the street, she went to the tiny shop that had once been Martin's watering hole and peered through the window. The faded red velvet curtain was ragged and the floor was dusty. No one had been inside for a while.

Ava started down the street. A woman wearing mirrored sunglasses brushed past her. Ava recognized her. It was the woman who had left the building Madame LeGris had entered on the rue Saint-André-des-Arts. Frowning at yet another coincidence, Ava watched the woman walk away.

"Ava!"

Hearing her name, Ava spun around. Jaspar was striding down the street toward her. He was a bundle of nerves. She had never seen him so nervous.

"Where's Martin?" Jaspar asked.

"He left."

"He just got here? Why did he leave?" Jaspar snapped before letting out a sigh. "Sorry. I'm not yelling at you. I've had a bad morning."

Ava shifted from foot to foot. "Martin left because our Simon Heppleworth is not his Simon Heppleworth. In fact, they are two different people." Seeing the confusion on Jaspar's face, she explained the situation as best she could.

Jaspar couldn't believe his ears. "Two Simon Heppleworths? Does the writer financing the film know that?"

"Martin had the same question," Ava said. "He even wondered if he was the wrong Martin."

Jaspar froze. "Don't tell me that there are two Martin Scotsdales!"

Seeing his reaction, Ava laughed. "As far as I know, there's only one. Unfortunately, it's our Martin Scotsdale. There's something else you need to know."

Jaspar remained silent, waiting for the other shoe to drop.

"Martin's first film was shot in Paris thirty years ago with the other Simon Heppleworth. And it was shot in the same mansion we're shooting in."

"As if I haven't had enough bad news today," Jaspar said as his shoulders slumped. "Let's go somewhere and get a drink."

They walked down to the rue Saint-André-des-Arts and headed up to the square near the Boulevard St. Michel. They sat down on the outside terrace of a bar in the shade of tall trees.

"First things first. Did Martin write the end?" Jaspar asked.

Ava nodded. "Like he told you on the phone, he's written it. He wants to tweak it some. He promised we'd have it first thing tomorrow morning."

Jaspar crooked his head and smiled. "Finally, something is going right."

The waiter arrived with two menus.

"I'll have a beer," Jaspar said. "What would you like, Ava?"

"A beer would be fine," Ava replied.

The waiter walked off.

Ava eyed Jaspar. He was so upset he looked like he was about to burst. "What's wrong?"

"I knew I couldn't fool you. The police called. We now know the identity of our dead man... George Maurel. He's a former jewel thief."

Ava felt like she'd been hit in the gut. "Does Henri know this?"

Jaspar shook his head. "Not yet. When I was at the set earlier, I told him about the note. The police only called an hour ago. They want to speak to everyone who was at the barge the day of the accident."

"What does it mean?"

Jaspar shrugged his shoulders. "Another coincidence. This whole film stinks to high heaven. I'd shut it down now, but it's too late for that. We've signed contracts and are on the line for the money. Lance and I would be sued if we stopped the film. Claiming that something nefarious is going on won't hold up in court. We'd need at least one or two more dead bodies for that."

A look of shock spread across Ava's face.

"Sorry. It was a joke," Jaspar said. "A bad joke."

The waiter arrived with their beers and a small bowl of potato chips.

Ava wrapped her hands around her glass. "What else did the police say?"

"Nothing," Jaspar replied. "However, Nate has a friend who's a police inspector. Nate called him. Our dead man has been out of circulation for a long time. He went to prison after a heist gone wrong twenty-five years ago and vanished after that. The man might be homeless as we suspected. However, the whiskey on the boat was very expensive, and the man was well-groomed."

"What do the police think happened?" Ava asked.

"An accident," Jaspar replied. "Unless they find something that makes them believe otherwise. I have no intention of leading them in that direction."

Ava sipped of her beer. A thought occurred to her. "Maybe the note is linked to something other than the dead man's death."

Jaspar broke a potato chip in two and ate it. "What do you mean?"

"The more we learn, the more coincidences there are. Maybe they aren't coincidences. Maybe the note was referring to something different. "

Jaspar shrugged as he sipped his beer. "I have no idea what's going on. I had it all wrong from the start." Contrite, he eyed Ava. "When I told you and Henri that I didn't know who the film's backer was, I was lying. I thought Martin was the writer and the backer."

Confused, Ava crinkled up her nose. "Why would you think that?"

"Martin Scotsdale is wealthy. He inherited the type of wealth that he could throw away on a vanity project like our film if he was the one who wrote the book. But after all you've told me, my theory doesn't hold water. Martin may be involved in what's going on, but he isn't the one financing the film," Jaspar said.

"Did you know that Martin's first film was shot in Paris?"

"No," Jaspar said. "I looked at his prior work. There was no mention of a film in Paris. Even though Simon said he didn't know Martin, I assumed that there was some back-story between them. Film is a small world. I thought they'd crossed paths somewhere, and that's why Martin wanted Simon hired. But as Martin isn't the one who's financing the film, that theory goes down the drain."

"I wonder if the person financing the film knows that they've hired the wrong Simon Heppleworth?" Ava asked.

"I have no idea what the person financing the film thinks. I'm incredulous that someone did finance it. Right now, I have a bad feeling. Since he saw the note this morning, Lance can barely function," Jaspar explained. "I certainly don't know who did it and after our discussion, I'm not even sure what "it" is."

"Maybe the note was meant for Simon or Martin," Ava said.

Jaspar knitted his brow. "I hadn't thought of that. Tell me about Martin."

"I can't see Martin killing anyone. What I found odd was how upbeat he was. You'd all warned me how unpleasant he could be. Before he learned about the two Simon Heppleworths, Paris seemed to have lifted his mood and chased away his bad memories."

"Bad memories?"

"His film came to a halt when Ken Waters, the director/producer vanished with the film's money. Martin's film, a tragic love story, was never finished. I can see where that upset him. But I can't see him staying away from Paris for thirty years because of that. Martin Scotsdale is made of stronger stuff," Ava explained. "There has to be more to the story than that. We need to discover what happened during the filming of that film."

"How can we do that? It was thirty years ago," Jaspar said.

Ava bit into a potato chip. "Could this tie in with Lance's late uncle?"

"Now I'm totally lost..." Jaspar said as he sipped his beer.

"Lance's uncle was a famous jeweler. Our dead man was a jewel thief. Lance's uncle left Paris thirty years ago. Martin's film was shot here thirty years ago."

"Coincidence is not causality," Jaspar replied.

"Who decided on the mansion?"

"Lance and I did, but Nate and the former location scout found it. There aren't a lot of mansions that fit with the story and were within our budget."

Ava fell silent. *Could Nate be involved? Is that why he got rid of the former location scout?*

"Plus, the mansion was perfect. It was almost as if the writer wrote the book to be shot there," Jaspar added.

"Maybe he did! Didn't you find the mansion's low price suspicious?" Ava asked.

"Ava, you're making this out to be some huge conspiracy. I agree something is going on, but that doesn't mean that everything is linked. Under your theory, I sent Loulou to your place to take photos."

Ava sighed. "You're right. I understand why conspiracy theories can become addictive... Everything fits perfectly like a puzzle."

"Except there is always a round peg that gets pushed through a square hole, and that's why people believe Elvis is still alive," Jaspar replied as he took a handful of chips.

Ava tapped her fingers on the table. "When I asked Martin if the mansion was haunted, he said it was and added that he didn't believe in ghosts. What could that possibly mean?"

"We'll have to ask him after we get the end of the script," Jaspar said. "Frankly, I'm astonished. The Martin you've described is not the drunk, belligerent entitled pain that I've been dealing with."

Ava smiled. "You see. Something good has happened!"

Jaspar looked down, ill at ease. "There's something else I should have told you and Henri from the start."

Ava had a sinking feeling in her stomach.

"I received an email two days ago telling me to stop the production. It was sent from my production company to my private email. My assistant didn't send it. The IP used was false," Jaspar said. "I'm sorry. I should have told you. I was hoping that you and Henri would discover that everything was fine."

"Was that why you were worried when you got the call in Café Zola?"

Jaspar nodded. "The moment I heard Nate's voice, I knew something was wrong. I just didn't know how wrong."

"Did you tell the police about the email when you spoke to them today?" Ava asked.

A look of alarm spread across Jaspar's face. "No."

Watching him, Ava sensed that Jaspar was still hiding something from her.

"Did you tell Nate about the email?" Ava asked.

"Yes. I didn't tell Lance though. That would send him over the deep edge."

"What did Nate say?" Ava asked.

"He thought it was a joke. Maybe he's right. It was a joke, and the email and the dead man aren't linked."

Ava pursed her lips. "Does Nate know that Henri and I are sleuths?"

"Absolutely not," Jaspar replied.

Ava was relieved. "Do they think the jewel thief was murdered?"

Jaspar gasped, astonished. "Murdered? No! I thought he met someone, they got drunk and he slipped. Murder means premeditation."

"Someone brought everyone together for the film," Ava said. "I find that suspicious. It's like the Agatha Christie book where everyone goes to an island."

"The one where they all die?" Jaspar asked, alarmed.

Ava nodded. "What are you going to do now?"

"Shoot the film. If Martin gives us the final scenes, Simon gets his act together and nothing else happens to throw us off schedule."

Ava took out her phone and went on the Internet.

"What are you doing?" Jaspar asked.

"Looking for Ken Waters." Ava typed in his name. There were hundreds of thousands of results for Ken Waters. She typed in "Ken Waters Paris film". There were zero results. She tried "Ken Waters Director". Again, there were zero results.

"Nothing?" Jaspar asked.

"It's as if he didn't exist."

"Thirty years ago was before the internet. Not everything from that time has been indexed."

"Who does the mansion belong to?" Ava asked.

"You'd have to ask Nate. A holding in Lichtenstein, I believe."

Ava frowned. Once again Nate's name had appeared. It was starting to become a habit. She'd have to try and find out more about him. "Who found the barge?" Ava asked.

"The ex-location scout. Why?"

"I heard it was cursed."

Jaspar burst out laughing. "I don't believe in ghosts. I don't believe in haunted mansions or cursed boats. If something is going on, it has to do with our world, not the spirit world."

Ava was inclined to agree with him. But her sleuthing experience has shown her that you should never eliminate something right out the gate. While Ava doubted that a ghost was involved, she couldn't entirely rule it out.

Jaspar's phone rang. "It's Nate." He answered. "Tell me. I'm listening." Jaspar's expression darkened. "I'll ring his neck if I get hold of him. I'll be right there."

"What is it?" Ava asked.

"Simon got in a fight with Claire, the assistant director. He accused her of leaving the barge unlocked and said that the man's death was her fault. Then fired her," Jaspar said.

"Can he do that?" Ava asked.

"No." Jaspar eyed Ava. "I was going to ask you out for dinner tonight, but it will have to be another night." He touched her hand, squeezed it awkwardly and signaled to the waiter for the check.

Despite everything that was going on, Ava was happy. As she watched Jaspar pay, she realized that Martin still didn't know about the dead man on the barge. She wondered what his reaction would be when he learned that.

CHAPTER 16

This is what happens when you answer a knock on your door on a rainy day,
Ava thought with a sigh as she plowed through the stack of
documents on the table before her in the production office.

What she wanted to do was discover what was going on. But
before she could put her sleuthing skills to the test, she had to
complete insurance documents, draw up the revised production
schedule, finish Henri's contract as well as any other number of
tasks that Nate had given her, and they all had to be finished by
tomorrow morning.

Ava was alone in the office. The crew had left early. Simon's
firing of Claire, the assistant director, had cast a pall over the
atmosphere. Despite Jaspar and Nate begging her to return, she
had refused. Her exact words were that she would return to the
production when "hell froze over".

After a long, animated discussion, Nate, Lance and Jaspar had gone to have dinner with Simon. It was an intervention dinner to convince him not to blow up the film. Ava guessed that was something Martin could do on his own without any help from the film's mercurial director.

Thinking of Martin, Ava checked the production company's email account as she had done several times already.

There was no sign of the script's final pages.

To be fair, Martin had said he would send them tomorrow morning. Ava sighed. With all she had to do, she would probably still be there when he sent them.

Ava's phone beeped. Flicking her head down, she eyed caller ID.

It was Henri.

She answered immediately. "You won't believe who the dead man was!"

Henri cut her off. "I ran into Jaspar at the mansion. He told me about the jewel thief. Is Jaspar there?"

"No. He, Lance and Nate left to have dinner with Simon."

"Probably begging him not to fire me," Henri joked.

"Give Simon time," Ava replied. "He'll find a way." There was something about Simon that rubbed her wrong. But she could say the same thing about Nate. Surprisingly, Ava liked Martin the best out of the three.

"What are you doing now?" Henri asked.

Ava looked at the stack of documents before her. "Living the dream life of making a film in Paris."

"Could you meet me on the Place Vendôme?"

"The Place Vendôme! Now?" Ava blurted out, startled. The Place Vendôme was a prestigious square in the first arrondissement. Close to the Louvre Museum and the Tuileries Garden, it was home to the Ritz Hotel, the French Justice Ministry and several high-end jewelry shops.

Was Henri getting delusions of grandeur?

"Henri, yesterday it was champagne, and today it's the Ritz?"

On the other end of the line, Henri chuckled. "Hardly. Although I will invite you and Jaspar to the Ritz when the film is completed. I managed to get in touch with a friend who knew Mr. LeGris. My friend is off to Hong Kong early tomorrow morning so it's now or never."

Ava looked at the work she had to finish. She pushed it aside. The documents could wait. Sleuthing came first. Lives depended on it. Besides, she could always come in at the crack of dawn to finish everything. "Where should we meet?"

"In front of Van Leptor and Company," Henri answered.

Ava caught her breath. Van Leptor and Company was the most expensive jewelry store in Paris. It was the high end of the high end. Billionaires and royalty wore Van Leptor jewels. "Can I go home and change?"

"There's no time for that, Ava. Come right away. I'll be waiting for you in front of the shop."

Twenty minutes later, Ava entered the Place Vendôme. Watching all the well-dressed people strolling about, she wished she had gone home to change. Clothes were very important in Paris. People judged you by what you were wearing. It wasn't the price tag that spoke the loudest, it was the style and sartorial choices that told people who you were.

Dismayed, Ava eyed her clothing.

She was dressed like someone who had been working on a film all day and hadn't had time to change.

As necessity was the mother of invention, Ava pushed her hair behind her ears, put on her favorite red lipstick and stood up straight. The right attitude was an antidote to anything.

True to his word, Henri was waiting in front of one of the shop windows of Van Leptor and Company. Henri's hair was still dark, but the mustache was gone. He was wearing elegant navy blue trousers, dark shoes and a white shirt that was so white it almost glowed.

"I got here as fast as I could," Ava said, striding up to him.

"Which bracelet do you prefer?" Henri asked, peering into the window.

Ava studied the window display. There were two bracelets in it. One was an exquisite sapphire and diamond bracelet. The other was a gold, diamond and mother of pearl bracelet.

Both were breathtaking.

"If I had to choose? I wouldn't. I'd take both. What do they cost?" Ava asked as she imagined herself sitting at her stand with diamond bracelets on both wrists.

Henri eyed the price list. The writing on it was so small that he had to squint. "The sapphire and diamond bracelet is 560,000 euros. The other bracelet is a mere 400,000. A bargain!"

"They're the price of a small Paris apartment," Ava protested in shock.

Henri nodded, unperturbed. In his former life as a notary, he was used to dealing with wealth. "They're perfect. The gems are of the highest quality. Skilled craftsmen carried out their design. If I'm not mistaken the sapphires are Kashmiri. Expensive? Absolutely. But the gems and craftsmanship are unparalleled."

Ava could only agree with him. "They are fabulous."

Henri looked at his watch. It was not the inexpensive watch he wore every day. It was his "notary" watch, an expensive Swiss watch that told the hour in three different cities and did everything except cook breakfast. "It's time for our meeting…"

Ava glanced at the bracelets one last time and followed Henri to the shop's front door.

The moment they stepped on the red carpet outside the door, an elegantly dressed broad-shouldered security guard politely blocked their way. "Van Leptor and Company is closed for the day," he said in a tone that indicated that anyone worth their salt would know that.

"Mr. Van Leptor is expecting us," Henri replied, totally at ease.

Hearing the magic words, the guard snapped to attention. With new spring in his step, he knocked on the door and nodded to a woman inside.

The woman buzzed Henri and Ava in.

The interior of Van Leptor and Company was exactly what Ava had expected. It was elegant, expensive and tasteful. The employees were emptying the display cases into velvet trays as an armed guard stood by. The employees were all dressed in simple well-cut clothing. None of the women wore jewelry.

But then how could they possibly compete with the jewelry in the window?

The woman who had buzzed them in dialed a number on the interphone. "Your guests are here."

"Send them up!" a deep male voice ordered.

Another woman appeared and led Henri and Ava to a private elevator. When they stepped inside, the doors closed automatically. The interior of the elevator was made of plush leather. Ava imagined that this was what wealth and privilege smelled like if wealth and privilege had an odor.

When the elevator doors opened on an upper floor, a short, plump man in his late sixties wearing bespoke tailoring and footwear strode toward them. He grasped Henri's hands in his, clearly delighted to see him. "Henri. This is an unexpected surprise. It's wonderful to see you. We should get together more often."

"I agree. But life intervenes," Henri said with a Gallic sigh.

"Ah, life," Mr. Van Leptor echoed, nodding his head in agreement.

Henri smiled at Ava. "This lovely woman is Ava Sext. She's Charles's niece."

Mr. Van Leptor's face lit up. "It's a pleasure to meet you. I wish your uncle could be here with us."

"Charles helped Mr. Van Leptor with a little problem," Henri explained to Ava.

"A little problem? A one million euro problem is in no way a little problem," Mr. Van Leptor said raising his eyebrows in indignation. "Your uncle did what was necessary, and he did it discreetly. I won't forget that. Please call me Guy. Whenever I hear Mr. Van Leptor, I expect my father to appear."

"Ava came directly from a film shoot and didn't have time to change," Henri said with a wave at her clothing.

A huge smile appeared on Guy's face. "Five years ago, a film company wanted to shoot in my shop. I was intrigued. The film had a famous American actor as its star. Unfortunately, common sense prevailed. The liability for us would have been off the charts. In the end, the production company copied the shop and built it in a studio. I did get a small cameo role though," Guy said with obvious delight.

Ava wondered if everyone in Paris had worked in film. Would she discover tomorrow morning at breakfast that Mercury had a day job as a famous animal actor?

"How can I help you?" Guy asked Henri.

"We need the wisdom of Paris's most famous jeweler," Henri replied.

"You flatter me," Guy said with a contented grin.

Henri shook his head. "Not at all. I'm just stating a fact. Ask anyone in Paris. They would tell you the same thing."

Guy led them into a private office. It was decorated in tones of beige and grey. A sitting area was in its center. The furniture was modern and elegant. Ava sank into an armchair and ran her hand over the leather armrest. The leather was as smooth as butter and smelled even more expensive than the leather in the elevator had. Henri sat next to Guy on a grey suede couch.

"After our conversation this afternoon, I went through my files," Guy said to Henri. "Louis LeGris... I hadn't heard his name in years. But then he was from my father's generation, not mine. I didn't go to LeGris's funeral service. It was a private affair."

"Madame LeGris is back in Paris," Henri said. "She's living in the mansion."

Guy pursed his lips. "I never met her. I don't know anyone who did. But she tamed the wild beast. Louis LeGris was a womanizer. Ladies loved him, and he loved them back. He was charming, wealthy and cultivated. He treated the women in his life like queens. Even when it was over, they still adored him. And then from one day to the next, he got married, left his jet-set life behind and moved to Switzerland. I can't say I was sorry. He was a serious competitor."

"LeGris wasn't on your level," Henri protested.

Guy shook his head. "His pieces weren't as perfect as ours.

However, LeGris had the ability to charm his way into the lives of extremely wealthy people and convince them to buy his jewels. No, that's unfair of me. They didn't need convincing. They wanted to buy jewels from him. They practically begged him to sell to them. Now tell me what's going on," Guy said as leaned forward, curious to know more.

"You heard about the death two days ago?" Henri asked.

"The death on the quay?" Guy replied with a knowing smile.

Ava's face showed her surprise.

Guy turned to her. "I follow closely anything that touches my profession. Friends keep me up to date."

Ava wondered if his friends belonged to the police.

Guy shook his head in admiration. "A jewel thief… The man who died belonged to a dying breed. No pun intended. Years ago, jewel thieves were people who understood and loved jewels. It was a point of pride for them that they stole the best and most perfect gems. Today, thieves are in it only for the money. They robbed the American of overpriced stones in cheap vulgar settings. It shows a complete lack of taste," Guy said, shaking his head in disapproval. "Now tell me how Louis LeGris is linked to the dead man."

"Madame LeGris's nephew is producing a film called *Death on the Quai*. It's about a jewel thief."

Deep in concentration, Guy kept his eyes on Henri. "Go on."

"The first set was a barge on the river. The dead jewel thief was found on that very same barge. The police believe it's an accident," Henri explained.

"But you don't?" Guy asked. Suddenly, he rose to his feet. "I'm forgetting my manners. What can I get you to drink? Whiskey, cognac?"

"Cognac," Henri said. "Cognac for Ava, also." He smiled at Ava. "You haven't drunk cognac until you've tried Guy's cognac."

"It's a weakness I inherited from my father," Guy said as he poured cognac into three cut crystal glasses. The light in the room jumped off the cuts in the crystal, making them shine like jewels. He handed a glass to Henri and Ava. "If you have the means to have the finest, then you should." Guy raised his glass in the air. "To the finest!"

Ava and Henri raised their glasses in the air.

"Spoken like a true revolutionary!" Henri teased as he sipped his cognac.

Guy grinned like a naughty schoolboy and eyed Ava. "Back in 1968, I was on the barricades. I was a foot soldier for the revolution. I wanted to overturn the capitalist system. But I grew up, began to work with my father and became accustomed to the finer things in life. It happens to even the most fervent revolutionaries. Look at Castro and his cigars!"

"Did you know the jewel thief?" Henri asked.

Guy swirled his cognac in his glass. "No. He was a small fry. He wasn't one of the big players. In the 70s and 80s, wealthy women flaunted their jewels. During the season, they went out decked from head to toe in diamonds, glistening like a Christmas tree. Our thief would help himself to an ornament or two every now and then. However, he only stole the finest. He was a small fry with an excellent eye."

"And the Countess Liccacio?" Ava asked. "Did you know her?"

"The countess?" Guy smiled in amazement. "I haven't thought of her in years. She had a mansion near the LeGris mansion. She would give fabulous balls in the winter. In the summer, she'd hold parties in her garden. Each season, she'd have a new protégé. But they were always men of talent. She was carrying on the tradition of being a patroness of the arts in her own way. They don't make women like that anymore. She had a fabulous jewel collection, absolutely unequaled at the time."

"*Death on the Quai* is being shot in her former mansion," Henri said.

A look of alarm spread across Guy's face. "I don't like that. I don't like that at all." He stood up and went over to a shelf behind his desk. He came back with a tablet. "We keep all the photos and press clippings about Van Leptor and Company in large albums. I had everything digitalized. It's easier to handle." He typed in the countess's name. Several photos appeared.

He stopped on one in which a stunning looking woman in her sixties was smiling at the camera. She was dressed in a white chiffon gown. A fabulous necklace hung from her neck. It had a huge emerald in its center. "The Tiger Emerald. It's rumored to be the same color as the eyes of a maharajah's favorite tiger."

Ava studied the photo. The Tiger Emerald was gorgeous.

Guy scrolled to another photo that had been taken at a ball. The countess was dressed in a black lace gown and was wearing the Tiger Emerald. She was speaking with an older man who looked exactly like Guy Van Leptor. "That's my father. The countess asked him to reset the emerald. My father was excited."

Henri raised his eyebrows. "With all due respect, Guy. I can't imagine your father getting excited about anything."

Guy shook his head. "The emerald was not anything. It was famous. It had a pedigree that went back 600 years. Legend has it that the jewel is cursed. If you stole it, you died. The countess inherited the jewel, so she was safe. Her father who had obtained the emerald under less than honest conditions had his throat slit on his yacht in Monte Carlo."

A shiver ran up Ava's spine. *A haunted mansion, a cursed barge and now a cursed jewel... What next?*

"Did your father reset it?" Henri asked.

"Unfortunately, no. It was one of the greatest regrets of his life. The countess said she'd changed her mind. It was rumored that the jewel had been stolen. You can imagine that we tried to find out more. Lips were sealed. No one knew anything. The countess never wore the emerald again, and it hasn't been seen since."

"When did this happen?" Henri asked.

Even before Guy responded, Ava knew the answer. "Thirty years ago?"

Guy nodded. "Thirty years ago."

"Around the time Louis LeGris left Paris…" Henri said.

"Around the time he left Paris," Guy confirmed with a curt nod. "But I can't see LeGris dealing with stolen gems. It wasn't his style."

"Who might have been involved?" Henri asked.

"On a heist like that?" Guy sipped his cognac, pensive. "The Riviera Gang comes to mind. They operated mainly in the south of France but occasionally came to Paris. The problem with a famous gem like that isn't stealing it, it's getting it off your hands. A lesser jewel would be easier to sell."

"The Riviera Gang? Could our jewel thief have been involved with them?" Henri asked.

Guy tilted his head to one side in thought. "He might have worked with them on one or two heists. I'd have to check. The gang was good at what they did. That's why they were famous. They were gentlemen thieves. No violence. No threats. They used intelligence and charm. The one time they were caught, the victim paid for their lawyers! The head of the gang retired to Rio de Janeiro and lived a long life." Guy scrolled through his tablet. "I have an article on the gang. An English reporter wrote about them. It was rumored that he even joined them on a heist to understand how they worked." He stopped at an article. "Here it is." Guy handed the tablet to Henri.

Henri read through the article. As he read, his features tightened. He handed the tablet to Ava. As she read, her face became flushed, and her heart began to beat faster.

It wasn't possible. It just wasn't possible.

Jaspar's father, Graham Porter, was the author of the article. Jaspar had never mentioned his father had written about jewel thieves. Ava checked the date. Jaspar would have been a young child when it was written. Still, this was a major story. Jaspar would have had to have known about it. *Why hadn't he told her?*

"Could you send me a copy of the article? Henri asked.

Guy nodded. "Is your email the same?"

"I'm a creature of habit," Henri replied.

"A creature of habit?" Guy burst out laughing. "My friend, that is not how I would describe someone who begins a new life as a bookseller at sixty!"

Henri smiled. "What happened after the countess changed her mind about resetting the jewel?"

Guy shrugged. "Nothing. She moved back to her palace in Rome. My father moved on to other jewels." Guy swirled his cognac. "If the jewel was stolen, LeGris was not the fence. If a link exists, it has to be subtler that that. Of course, for a famous jewel like that he might have gone against his principles. I have a hard time envisioning that. No, the answer lies elsewhere."

"Did Madame LeGris know the countess?" Ava asked.

Guy frowned. "Why do you ask?"

"Maybe Louis LeGris had a dalliance with the countess. If that were the case, he might have left Paris to keep his jealous wife happy."

"Love could have played a role. After all, LeGris was French. Somehow, I doubt it's that simple. If you find the Tiger Emerald, promise me that you'll let me know."

Henri smiled. "That goes without saying."

"What is the Tiger Emerald worth now?" Ava asked.

"To someone like me, it's priceless. On the market... maybe

five million euros," Guy responded.

A look of astonishment spread across Ava's face.

"Perfection has its price. Let me show you." Guy stood up and went to a small wall safe. He unlocked it, took out a small box and carried it over. He opened the box and placed the green stones inside it on a black velvet tray on the table. He handed the tray to Ava. "These emeralds took millions of years to reach this state of perfection. They were hidden in rocks deep inside the mountains of Zimbabwe and Brazil. Men battled the elements, disease and violence to wretch them from their home. Some men probably died for them. But the gems continued on. They were cut and polished and are worth a small fortune today."

Ava studied the stones. There was something almost mystical about their journey from the depths of the earth to the Place Vendôme.

Guy continued. "A stone like the countess's emerald has a story linked to it. It's that story that separates it from other emeralds of the same quality. Five million euros is a small price to pay for a jewel that is the same color as the eyes of the maharajah's tiger."

Sensing the meeting had come to an end, Henri rose to his feet. "We won't keep you any longer."

Guy stood up and walked Ava and Henri to the elevator. "I'll ask around discretely to see if I can discover anything else." He turned to Ava and grinned. "Like your uncle, I like to solve mysteries."

Ava was silent as they left Van Leptor and Company. Stepping out onto the Place Vendôme, she turned to Henri. "Was the jewel thief killed because of the Tiger Emerald?"

"I assume so. The thief is linked to what is going on. Unfortunately, he's dead and won't be able to tell us what that link is or why people are trying to find the jewel after all this time. It's no coincidence that *Death on the Quai* is about a jewel heist," Henri said. "It's strange that Jaspar didn't mention his father's article."

Remembering Jaspar touching her hand tenderly, Ava felt a wave of pain rush through her. For some reason, Jaspar didn't trust her. But then why should he? They hadn't seen each other in years.

As if reading Ava's mind, Henri stared at her with concern. "I don't know why Jaspar didn't tell us about his father, but he must have his reasons. We have to find out what those reasons are. Where is his father?"

"Somewhere in Asia. When Jaspar emailed him to say was coming to Paris to work on a film, his father said he was too busy to come."

Henri raised his eyebrows. "Was Jaspar surprised by that?"

Ava shook her head. "Surprised? No. Was he disappointed?

Yes. When I worked on his student film, Jaspar often joked if he wanted to see his father, he'd have to turn on the television."

The expression on Henri's face became serious. "We need to find out more about the jewel. I have a friend who works at Lloyds of London. A jewel of that price would have had to have a syndicate insuring it. Thirty years ago, Lloyds would have been the insurer of choice. If the dead thief was after the Tiger Emerald, I fear he won't be the only death."

"Jaspar didn't do it!" Ava blurted out. Immediately, she was embarrassed.

"I agree with you. However, he might know something he's not telling us for his own reasons." Henri said.

Ava wished she could disagree with Henri. "How are Martin, Simon and the film linked to the jewel?"

"Martin knew the countess. Simon's late cousin knew her, too. Louis LeGris certainly met her. She was a rich socialite, and they were neighbors."

"What am I going to tell Jaspar?" Ava asked.

"Nothing until we discover what he's hiding."

Ava fell silent. As much as she wanted to disagree with Henri, she knew he was right. Jaspar was hiding something, and she intended to find out what that was. Standing there, a plan popped into her mind. It was time to do some sleuthing.

CHAPTER 17

Alone in the production office, Ava focused on her work. After leaving the Place Vendôme, she had headed directly to Catastrophe Productions. She needed to complete her tasks before she implemented her plan. As she worked, she pushed Jaspar, the countess, Martin, Simon and the Tiger Emerald to the back of her mind.

First things first…

Two hours later, she watched with satisfaction as the production schedules for the week came out of the printer. She stacked them up and placed them next to three copies of Henri's contract and the rest of the work she had completed.

She looked around the empty office and took a deep breath. It was time for her real work to begin.

She had deliberately not informed Henri of her plan. He would have discouraged her, saying it was foolhardy and possibly dangerous, and he would have been right.

But the story of the stolen jewel and Jaspar's father meant that drastic measures were necessary. She didn't want to fall in love with a man who might be a killer. Her late uncle had often said that murderers became more dangerous with time.

If a murderer got away with one murder, why not two?

After verifying that the office's front door was locked, Ava placed a small metal trashcan in front of it. If someone did enter the office, the door would hit the can and make a noise that would alert her to the person's presence.

Resolute, Ava headed back to the scene of the crime: the office where the note had been found that morning.

Entering the dark room, she flicked on the light and moved to the bulletin board. Although the note was long gone, Ava could still see it hanging there in her mind's eye.

What did the note mean?

Standing there, Ava realized that she had spent much of the day wondering if Lance, Nate or Jaspar had done it. But the note had said "you know who did it", not "you did it".

That might mean that the person or persons the note was intended for knew who had killed the jewel thief or they might know who had stolen the emerald. And that was just the start.

Ava knitted her brow as other possibilities came to mind.

It could also mean that the person the note was intended for knew why the writer was financing the film. The person might even know how Simon and Martin's back-stories were linked or why Louis LeGris had left Paris. The note writer might even be the author of the book and the film's backer!

However, there was another possibility... The note's author knew nothing and had put the note on the board to shake people up. If that was the author's intention, he or she had succeeded. The note had visibly disturbed Lance, Jaspar and Nate.

Ready to put her plan into action, Ava eyed the three desks before her.

She chose Lance's desk to search first as the production office belonged to his company.

Like earlier, Lance's desk was a hymn to chaos. Bills were piled on top of empty candy wrappers. Photos of the countess's mansion spilled out of a plastic bag. There were drawings for a storyboard. Different versions of the script were annotated in red and green marker. A cryptic post-it on the cover of one of them read: You can do it.

Ava frowned.

Do what? The murder? *Lance?* Impossible.

The post-it might be referring to the film. With all that was happening, Ava doubted that Lance could produce the film on his own. However, Jaspar and Nate could. Even if both men were after the jewel, they would keep the film on track. If Simon and Martin didn't screw it up, *Death on the Quai* would begin shooting in two days.

Suddenly, Ava froze.

Maybe the writer had no intention of funding the film to the end. Would the money stop when the emerald was found?

Frustrated that she hadn't found a smoking gun in Lance's papers, Ava walked over to Jaspar's desk and settled into his chair. She eyed his desk, loath to go through his papers. Not only had Jaspar hired her, he was an old friend and a future romantic interest. She was not the sort of woman who searched through a love interest's phone or computer.

She reminded herself that the search wasn't personal. It was professional. She had to discover what was going on before there was another death.

To her relief, hunting through Jaspar's desk was a breeze. Everything was well organized. His papers were divided into folders. There was a TO DO file, a TO FILE file, and a TO LOOK AT file. There was nothing about his father or a jewel in any of them. She was also happy that there were no photos of girlfriends or anything linking him to the thief's death.

More determined than ever, she swirled around in Jaspar's chair, stood up and approached Nate's desk.

Whereas both Jaspar and Lance had some link to jewels, Nate had none. He was just the production manager.

Ava instantly regretted the term "just".

Being a production manager required an incredible amount of hard work, stamina and intelligence. Nate was the person who kept all the balls in the air no matter what happened. That took talent and perseverance to pull off. Nate had all of that and more.

Nate's papers were neatly piled up. Taking care to put the papers back exactly as she found them, she searched through his desk. She suspected that Nate would know someone had gone through his papers. Her brief experience with him had shown her that he was very intuitive.

At the bottom of Nate's papers, Ava found a copy of an article on the Countess Liccacio and her jewels. Stunned, Ava read it. It spoke about the Tiger Emerald and its curse. So Nate knew about the jewel. He had been the one to find the barge and the mansion. Was he doing it in an attempt to find the jewel?

There was only one way to find out what was going on. She had to proceed with part two of her plan, no matter how risky it was. She had to go back to the scene of the crime... the original crime.

While she had no proof that the Tiger Emerald had been stolen, she sensed that it was at the center of whatever was going on.

Taking a deep breath, she strode to the key rack on the wall and eyed the keyrings hanging there.

There were keys to the barge, keys to the production office, keys to the production vehicles, keys to the LeGris mansion and keys to the countess's mansion. Ava knew this because each key set was clearly labeled. She reached for the keys to the countess's mansion.

If the mansion was haunted, she would soon find out. And if it wasn't, she would discover why people thought it was.

The haunting wasn't something new. Martin had said that even the countess had believed that her mansion was haunted. However, he has also said that he didn't believe in ghosts.

Until Ava met one, she, too, would remain skeptical.

Stuffing the keys in her pocket, she left the office, turning out the lights behind her. She checked the production email one last time to see if Martin had sent the end of the script. She wasn't at all surprised to see that he hadn't.

Stepping into the courtyard, she gazed at the LeGris mansion. It was dark. Its shutters were closed. There was no sign of Lance or the mysterious Madame LeGris.

Ava went through the coach doors and hurried down the street toward the countess's mansion. Despite it being a Friday night, the neighborhood was quiet. The distant sound of music and laughter wafted down from the rue Saint-André-des-Arts. As Ava walked down the silent street, her heart began to beat louder.

When she passed by the small triangular building that had once been a bar, she thought she saw a faint light at the edge of the curtain. Ava walked up to the glass window and pressed her face against it, trying to see inside. The faded red velvet curtain blocked her view. Everything was now dark. She listened but heard nothing.

Maybe the bar's haunted, too, Ava thought with a smile.

When she reached the countess's mansion, she unlocked the coach doors and entered the courtyard. In the darkness, the snack tent looked funereal, and the olive trees resembled gnarled gnomes from a fairy tale.

Everything was silent.

But it was a noisy silence where you heard your heart beat, and the slightest breeze howled loudly.

Ava stood there and waited.

What was she waiting for? A sign to continue…

Creeping around a haunted mansion alone at night was not a good idea. Standing there, it struck her that given that there had already been one death, it was an especially bad idea.

When no bolt from the heavens came telling her what to do, she threw her shoulders back and whispered her late uncle's maxim: Never reverse a decision because of fear.

Striding to the mansion's front door, she unlocked it and entered the entrance hall. In the dark, danger seemed to lurk in every corner.

Trying to keep her fear in check, she took out her cell phone and turned its flashlight on. The light was swallowed up by the blackness, but it revealed enough that she could move without hurting herself.

She started to the steps that led to the upper floor. Gazing out at the garden, she halted. Unlocking the garden door, she went outside. The tall trees cast a heavy darkness over everything. The darkness was so black that it was almost physical. The odor of the gardenias and angel's trumpet -- both night flowers -- was overwhelming and accentuated her feeling of danger. She eyed the LeGris mansion. It was dark except for a light on the top floor. Looking up, Ava sensed someone was staring at her. Instantly, she stepped inside.

She was now filled with a sense of urgency. If the person at the LeGris mansion was Lance, he might come and investigate.

Following her phone's faint light up the stairs, Ava made her way to the landing. Reaching it, she stopped, uneasy. She waved her flashlight around. Its light danced off the walls, but it didn't reveal anything or anyone.

A shiver ran up her spine.

Her sleuthing sixth sense was telling her that she wasn't alone. Someone else was there!

She tiptoed to the door of the reception hall and pushed it open.

The enormous room was cast in darkness. As she stood there, she heard a faint noise coming from the sitting room at its far end.

Ava froze. At first, she thought it was her imagination playing tricks on her. She held her breath and listened. After a few seconds, she heard the noise again.

Someone was there!

Turning off her flashlight, she inched forward, her heart beating a mile a minute. If it was a ghost, she'd have stories to tell her grandchildren. If it wasn't, she was walking into danger.

Reaching the far end of the room, she peered through the partly open door into the sitting room. Ava could hear someone moving about.

She remained immobile and waited.

After what seemed like an eternity, a figure walked past the door. It was so dark, Ava couldn't make out who it was. The figure went to the wall and began pressing on it.

As her eyes adjusted to the darkness, Ava saw that it was a man. When he moved to the fireplace and began to run his hands over the panels around it, she recognized the man's silhouette.

It was Jaspar.

Jaspar was searching the countess's mansion. He was looking for the emerald.

Had he killed for it?

Ava bit her lip. Jaspar might be a liar looking for a jewel, but he wasn't a killer. That afternoon, he had speculated that the jewel thief's death might have been an accident. She hoped it was. In fact, she prayed it was.

Before she could decide whether to confront him or not, Jaspar walked to the countess's dressing room and entered it, closing the door behind him.

Ava crept into the sitting room. As she moved toward the dressing room door, she heard the sound of footsteps coming across the reception hall. Instinctively, she moved to a closet she had seen in the room earlier that day. When she opened its door to slip inside, there was movement next to her. Before she could turn, a hand shoved her into the closet.

"Stay there!" a voice whispered.

Ava stood in the dark closet, terrified. *What was going on? Who was there?* She expected to hear a gunshot or shouting. Instead, she only heard silence. Sliding to the floor, she waited. Finally, she took her courage in hand, cracked the door open and peered out.

All she saw was darkness. There was no sign of anybody.

Opening the door wider, she stepped out into the sitting room. It was dark and silent. As her heart beat loudly, Ava moved toward the dressing room door and pushed it open.

The dressing room was dark.

In one bold move, Ava swung the door wide-open, stepped inside and looked around.

A figure appeared. Before Ava could react, the bright light of a flashlight hit her in the eyes, blinding her.

"Can I ask you what you're doing here in the middle of the night?" a familiar voice asked.

Ava stared out at Nate. She didn't have an answer, but she knew she had to find one quickly.

CHAPTER 18

The kitchen of the countess's mansion looked like it had come directly from a magazine ad for luxury kitchens. It was a perfect example of good taste and unlimited funds. The walls and cabinets were in different shades of dove grey. The rest of the fittings had a dull silver metallic finish. An ultra-modern pale grey marble island throned in the center of the kitchen. Ultramodern designer stools circled it.

Standing at the marble island, Nate poured boiling water from an electric kettle into two cups with tea bags in them. He handed Ava a cup. "Do you want honey or sugar to go with your tea?"

"Honey," Ava responded as she shifted on her stool.

Nate went to a cabinet and took a jar of organic honey out. "The kitchen is fully stocked even though no one has lived here for years. There's even fresh milk and butter in the refrigerator. I guess the rich are different. Their homes are ready for them even if they never use them."

Ava took a spoonful of honey and put some in her tea. She stirred vigorously in an attempt to avoid Nate's probing eyes as he slid onto a stool across from her.

"Now can you tell me what you're doing here in the middle of the night?" Nate asked.

Debating whether to tell him the truth or lie, Ava opted for a lie. "I left my keys here this afternoon. I came by to get them."

Nate stared at her. "Why didn't you turn the lights on?"

"I could ask you the same thing," Ava said, combative. She had no intention of mentioning Jaspar until she knew more. That limited the possible subjects of discussion.

Nate ran his hand through his thick hair. "I came here to think about the film. I heard a noise. If it was a ghost, I intended to catch it. Instead, I found you creeping around."

"Creeping! I wasn't creeping. I was moving quietly," Ava protested. "I heard a noise. I was so frightened that I hid in a closet. When I came out, you appeared!"

"Did you find your keys?" Nate asked.

Ava took her keychain out of her pocket and dangled it in the air. "Yes, I did. Thank you."

Nate sipped his tea and stared at Ava. "Let's start at the beginning. How did you get to Paris so quickly? When I spoke with Jaspar's assistant the morning we found the body, she said she was coming."

"Loulou!" Ava responded, happy to change the subject.

Puzzled, Nate raised his eyebrows. "Loulou Pleyel?"

Ava nodded. "She came to take pictures of my tower for a possible roof top scene. I worked on a film with Jaspar ages ago in London. When he saw me in Loulou's pictures, he asked me to work on the film. His assistant didn't want to leave her cat."

"I can understand that," Nate said, cracking a smile. "For a moment, I thought Jaspar was dating you."

Ava raised her eyebrows in protest. "Jaspar is an old friend. We've known each other for years."

"What's your impression of Martin?" Nate asked out-of-the-blue.

"Martin?" Ava was pensive. "He made his first film here in this mansion."

Nate nodded. "Jaspar told me about that. I'm trying to find out more about the production and the director. I've worked in film for years and know a lot of people. Someone is bound to know someone who worked on Martin's film. They might even know the other Simon."

Ava's eyes lit up. She was excited to hear this. She sensed that Martin's film held the key to what was going on.

"How did Martin seem to you this afternoon? Was he upset or angry?" Nate asked.

Ava thought back to her encounter with the irascible screenwriter. "Nostalgic. If anything, he was nostalgic. He was also filled with regret."

With an inscrutable look on his face, Nate leaned toward Ava. His grey eyes stared straight at her. "Regret about what?"

Ava shifted on her stool to escape Nate's stare. "That he hadn't come to Paris in thirty years, that he'd been afraid of the past when there wasn't anything to be afraid of…"

Nate nodded. "Did he tell you what his film was about?"

Ava smiled. "It's the oldest story on earth… a love story. Boy meets girl. Girl meets another boy. Things become complicated. She kills herself. Martin said that if he wrote the same script today, he would have ended it with her staying alive."

"What was his reaction when he arrived at the mansion?" Nate asked as he sipped his tea.

"At first, he was in a daze. He feared that the past was waiting for him. But as he walked through the mansion, his mood lightened. He realized that the past was just the past and that there was nothing to fear. It was a liberation of sorts for him."

Nate listened carefully as if trying to fit her words into a narrative that he was building in his mind.

"He showed us the countess's sitting room and dressing room. You can still smell her violet perfume in the closets," Ava said with a smile.

"Did he say anything about the film's director?" Nate asked.

"Ken Waters? Only that he was a ladies' man who had convinced the countess to finance the film. Ten days into the shoot, Ken took the money and vanished. Martin was crushed. His dream ended prematurely."

Nate nodded. "A first film is important. Having it come crashing down around you would be devastating. What happened when Martin met Simon?"

Ava ran over the encounter between the two men. With each word, Nate's expression darkened.

Nate stood up and began to pace around the kitchen. "Was Martin upset that Simon was the wrong Simon?"

With each question about Martin, Ava began to suspect that something lay behind Nate's interest in the man.

"At first, he was angry and astonished. Then he found it curious. He wondered if Simon was the wrong Simon. And if he was, what did that mean?" Ava explained. "He also wondered if he was the right Martin?"

"The right Martin? What does that mean?" Nate said with a quizzical look on his face.

Ava shrugged. "You'll have to ask Martin. He also believes that the person financing the film is up to something."

Nate frowned. "Did he tell you what that was?"

"No. Martin appears to have no idea who the film's backer is," Ava added.

"Did he tell you how *Death on the Quai* ends?" Nate asked.

"No. We'll have to wait until tomorrow morning. He promised we'd have the last pages then." Suddenly, Ava remembered something. "I didn't tell him about the death on the barge. I was worried about his reaction."

Nate leaned against the counter. His features were tense as if he were hiding something.

Ava stared at him. "Is there something I should know?"

"When we went to have dinner with Simon, he didn't show up or answer his phone. As Simon's apartment was right around the corner from the restaurant, Jaspar went to see if he was there. The door was open. Simon was sitting on the floor, dazed. When he went back to his apartment before dinner, someone was searching it. The person pushed Martin. He fell, hit his head and passed out."

"Did he see who it was?" Ava asked, horrified.

"No," Nate replied.

"We called Martin's place. He didn't answer the phone," Nate said. "That doesn't mean it was Martin."

"Did you call the police?" Ava asked.

Nate's eyebrows shot up. "Absolutely not! Simon insisted on that. We agreed with him. He doesn't want to do anything that would slow down shooting. No matter what happens, this film will be made.

"Is that a good idea?" Ava asked.

"It's not an idea. It's a fact. We're going to make the film."

"What was Lance's reaction?" Ava asked as she remembered his panicked reaction to the note.

"He fell apart," Lance admitted.

"Poor Lance. Maybe he should have named his film company *Miracle Productions*," Ava said with a sigh.

Nate smiled. "I like Lance. He's just not made to be a producer. He spends half his time telling Simon how he would shoot the film if he were the director."

"Maybe Simon's attacker believed he was the other Simon," Ava suggested.

"That's a possibility. It might also be that the attacker thought Simon knew something about the countess's jewels."

Ava went white. For an instant, she didn't speak. She was astonished that he admitted that he knew about them. "Why do you think that?"

Nate ticked off the reasons on his fingers. "One. *Death on the Quai* is about a jewel heist. Two. We found a dead jewel thief on our set. Three. The countess who owned this mansion was known for her fabulous jewel collection including an emerald called the Tiger Emerald. Four. Someone wrote the book *Death on the Quai* and is financing the film. It's a banal story. Why finance it? I suspect the writer's reason for financing it -- if it is the writer who is financing it as we have no proof of that except the lawyer's word -- isn't to get *Death on the Quai* into the Cannes Film Festival. As for five, I'll have to sleep on it." Nate stood up. "It's late. I'm going to call a taxi for you.

"What are you going to do?" Ava asked.

"Hang around and wait for the ghost. Maybe he or she will have the answer to what's going on." Nate eyed Ava. "Before I came here, I stopped by the production office. I didn't expect you to finish everything tonight."

"You said it was for tomorrow morning. By my estimation, tomorrow morning is fast approaching. When I have work to do, I do it," Ava replied.

Nate smiled. "That's a rare quality. Now that your work is done, sleep in late tomorrow. We'll be expecting you after lunch and not a moment sooner."

Nate took out his phone to call a taxi. As he dialed, Ava studied him. She wondered what he really was doing in the countess's mansion. She suspected it had very little to do with thinking about the film or ghost hunting.

CHAPTER 19

The telephone rang. It rang again. Half asleep, Ava opened her eyes. The sun was streaming through the glass roof overhead. Panicked, she fumbled for the phone and answered it.

"Ava," Henri said.

Ava sat up. "Am I late?"

"Not at all. I'd like to postpone our meeting until 10:30. Is that OK?"

"Perfect," Ava said as she slipped under the covers and closed her eyes.

Wide-awake after three coffees and an icy shower, Ava hurried down the rue des Saints-Pères toward the Seine. She was anxious to see Henri and tell him everything that had happened at the countess's mansion the night before. Events were accelerating, and she still was clueless as to what was going on. Hopefully, Henri would be able to shine a light on the situation.

Glancing at her reflection in one of the shop windows that lined the street, Ava was happy at what she saw. She was wearing a chic sleeveless blue T-shirt dress and had brushed her long hair until it shone. A touch of makeup gave her a healthy, natural glow. Luckily, Mercury was long gone when she had gotten up so she didn't have to deal with his judgmental stare. After yesterday's visit to the Place Vendôme, Ava had decided she'd rather be an overdressed production assistant than an underdressed sleuth.

When she reached Café Zola, it was almost empty. Gerard raised his eyebrows when she walked up to the counter. Like a doctor, he studied her before giving his professional opinion on what she should order. "Café crème and a croissant!"

"Café crème, two croissants and a hard-boiled egg," Ava replied.

Gerard grinned. "Your wish is my command. Henri called to say he's on his way."

Ava grabbed the local paper off the counter and headed to Henri's table in the back of the café. As she settled into the red leather bench against the wall, she paged through the paper. Once again, the pages were full of details about the theft of the American star's jewels. There was a mention of the death of a former jewel thief on a barge on the Seine. However, the article dismissed the possibility that the death was linked to the theft of the American's jewels.

It was another lucky break for the film.

Ava checked the horoscope for Aquarius. It said she would have a productive day. Productive was a little vague. But as long as her horoscope didn't threaten fire and brimstone, she was fine. Whatever she discovered today, she would deal with it. All she needed was to focus her mind and keep her imagination in check... two things that were easier said than done.

Putting her hand in her pocket, she pulled out two sets of keys and put them on the table. The first set were the keys to Martin's place. She had forgotten to leave them at the production office. The second set were the keys to the countess's mansion. She would stop by the locksmith and make a copy. That way she could put them back on the key rack in case anyone else wanted to make a late night visit.

Like Jaspar?

Ava chided herself. Before jumping to conclusions about his actions, she had to allow him to explain.

Another unwelcome thought popped into her mind... Why had Jaspar been the one to go to Simon's apartment?

A whole range of explanations came to mind... Maybe Jaspar was the one who had pushed Simon. He had gone back to cover his tracks. It was also possible that Simon and Jaspar were in this together, and the fall had been faked. Perhaps the true reason Jaspar had asked her and Henri for help was so that he could find the Tiger Emerald in an attempt to live up to his father's reputation.

Ava sighed. For someone who had just vowed to keep her imagination in check, she was off to a rocky start.

"You're right on time," Henri said with approval as he slipped into the chair across from her.

"We have a lot to talk about. First, I have a confession. After I finished at the production office last night, I went to the countess's mansion," Ava admitted with a guilty nod. "I should have told you. I'm sorry."

Henri smiled. "I expected you would."

Astonished, Ava sat up straight as an arrow. "You expected that I'd go there in the middle of the night?"

"Let's say I'm not surprised."

Ava's eyebrows shot up. "Why didn't you try and stop me?"

"Would it have worked?" Henri asked.

"Probably not," Ava said.

All-ears, Henri leaned toward her. "Now tell me what happened. Did you see a ghost?"

Before Ava could respond, Gerard arrived.

"A double espresso for Henri. A large café crème for Ava and croissants for both of you," Gerard said as he placed a basket of crispy croissants on the table. With a smile, he put a plate in front of Ava. "A special omelet with fresh herbs."

Ava's eyes lit up as he set the plate in front of her. "You didn't have to do that. A hard-boiled egg would have been fine."

Gerard shook his head. "After what you've been through, you needed something hot to start the day."

Ava was astonished. "How did you know that something happened?"

Gerard shook his head. "I could tell by the expression on your face."

Looking at the omelet, Ava felt her taste buds awakening. "Thank you, Gerard. What would I do without you?"

Content, Gerard smiled and left.

"What did you see at the mansion?" Henri asked as he sipped his espresso.

"No ghosts… But someone was there," Ava replied.

"Who was it?" Henri asked as his eyes bored into her.

Ava lied. "I'm not sure." Her lie was a spur of the moment decision. She had to give Jaspar a chance to explain his presence at the mansion before she revealed it to Henri. "It was dark. I was spooked. I'm pretty sure it was a man. I only saw the person's back."

"Any idea who it was?" Henri asked as casually as possible.

Ava shook her head. "No."

Henri kept his eyes on her. "What was the man doing?"

Uneasy, Ava took a croissant. "He was running his hands over the walls and the molding around the fireplace in the sitting room."

Henri sipped his coffee. "And then?"

"He went into the dressing room and closed the door. I heard footsteps coming from the reception room. Before I could react, someone stepped out of the dark and shoved me into the closet."

Henri's expression was a mix of alarm and bewilderment. "There were three people there?"

Ava nodded. "I don't know who they were. I stayed in the closet for an eternity. When I came out, everything was silent. I crept over to the dressing room door, opened it and a flashlight blinded me."

Henri watched her.

Wondering if he knew she was lying about Jaspar, Ava looked away. "It was Nate."

Henri's face showed his astonishment. "Nate? What was he doing there?"

"He wanted to think about the film." Ava's eyes opened wide. "I almost forgot to tell you the most important!"

Henri caught his breath. "There's more?"

"Simon was attacked," Ava announced.

Suddenly, Henri was all business. "Where?"

"In his apartment. He went back there before dinner. When he opened the door, someone was there. The person pushed him. Simon fell and lost consciousness. When Simon didn't arrive at the restaurant or answer his phone, Jaspar went to his apartment and found him."

"Did they call the police?" Henri asked.

Ava shook her head. "After the death on the quay, they decided that would be a bad idea. Everyone wants the film to start shooting tomorrow."

Henri pursed his lips, deep in concentration. "Maybe that isn't a good idea…"

"Nate knows about the Tiger Emerald. I found an article on the countess and the emerald on his desk, and he mentioned it when we spoke."

Henri took a croissant. "Nate is smart and inquisitive. We'll have to keep our eyes on him. What did he say when he found you?"

"I told him that I'd forgotten my keys. He didn't believe me. Maybe he thought I was a ghost hunter," Ava joked.

"Be careful, Ava," Henri warned.

"I'm not falling under his spell." As soon as the words came out of her mouth, Ava wondered if she was falling under Nate's spell.

Perplexed, Henri stared at her. "I didn't mean that. Don't forget that Nate was the one who found the body. We have to suppose that he was looking for the jewel at the mansion unless he has other motives we don't know about."

Ava's eyes widened. "Madame LeGris! I saw her on my way to Martin's place. She got out of a car and entered a building on the rue Saint-André-des-Arts. When she didn't come out, I slipped inside and took photos of the names on the mailboxes."

Henri smiled in approval. "You are certainly very intrepid."

Ava didn't know if he was teasing her or not. "I'm a Sext, Henri. We're all intrepid." She pulled up the photos and handed her phone to Henri.

Concentrated, he scrolled through them. "There are no names here that are familiar."

"I know," Ava said with disappointment. "If this were a mystery novel, the key to everything would be one of the names on the mailbox. Instead, it's another dead end.

"There is a dentist and an acupuncturist on the list. Maybe Madame LeGris was seeing one of them," Henri suggested as he scrolled back through the photos.

"I'd hoped it was a lover," Ava said in a wistful tone.

Henri burst out laughing. "You're starting to sound French."

"There's something else I had wrong. The note said: You know who did it. It didn't say: You did it. I spent much of yesterday wondering which of them did it when I should have focused on who each one might be protecting," Ava admitted

"Like Jaspar protecting his father?" Henri asked, eyeing her.

"Like Jaspar protecting his father. Or Lance protecting his late uncle," Ava quickly added. "Lance is indebted to him. He might want to keep the LeGris name pure."

Henri nodded. "Lineage counts for a lot in France, although even the best families have rogues in them. Mr. LeGris is dead. Who would care if he dealt in stolen jewels years ago?"

"Lance would. Also, if his uncle's reputation was blackened, it might upset Madame LeGris. Lance is devoted to her."

"I hadn't thought of that," Henri said. "And Nate?"

Ava shrugged. "I don't know him well enough to say who he'd protect or not. My guess is that he wants to protect the film. He takes great pride in seeing a film to the end."

"Who hired him?"

"Jaspar," Ava replied.

Henri was silent.

"You think they're working together?" Ava asked. *Had Nate gone there to meet Jaspar? If that was the case, who pushed her in the closet?*

"I don't know what to think yet," Henri confessed.

"The "yet" worried Ava. She feared Henri had started to suspect Jaspar.

Henri took a second croissant and bit into it. "I postponed our meeting this morning so I could get more information from my friend at Lloyds of London. As I suspected, they did insure her jewels. While the countess never made a claim for the Tiger Emerald, she did stop insuring it. She didn't give Lloyds a reason for that decision."

Ava raised her eyebrows. "Let me guess. She stopped insuring it around the time Martin's film was being made."

Henri nodded.

"Has anyone insured the jewel since?" Ava asked.

"Not that my friend knows of. It might be that the new owner doesn't want anyone to know they own it," Henri explained.

"So it wasn't stolen?" Ava asked, puzzled.

"If it was, the countess didn't report it."

"Then what is this all about?" Ava asked, taking another croissant.

"You're hungry?" Henri asked.

"I didn't have dinner last night. When I got home, I was too tired to eat."

Henri burst out laughing. "Too tired to eat? That's not French."

"There's something else. I thought I saw a light in the small triangle bar last night."

Henri frowned. "The vacant shop outside the mansion walls?"

Ava nodded. "The very same."

"You're sure it wasn't a ghost?" Henri teased.

Ava was annoyed that he wasn't taking her seriously. "What are we going to do?"

"You still have the mansion keys?"

Ava pointed to them. "I'm going to make a copy before I go to the office."

"We'll go there tonight," Henri announced.

"Something's going to happen?" Ava asked, excited.

"The film starts shooting tomorrow night. If you wanted to find the jewel, this is the last time things will be calm for a while."

"I hope you saved me a croissant," Ali, the artist who ran the stand next to Ava's stand, said as he joined them. He had a "cat that ate the canary" expression on his face.

"To what do we owe this honor?" Ava asked Ali.

Ali raised his eyebrows and gave them a conspiratorial look. "I have the lowdown on the barge. Yesterday evening, I went down to the police boat and chatted with the captain again. He called his predecessor, the one who told him that the barge was cursed." Ali stopped talking and took a croissant.

"What did he say? What did you find out?" Ava asked.

"The barge caught on fire years ago. They found a dead man and woman on it. The police never identified them. No one was reported missing. The police thought it was backpackers coming through Paris. They often squatted the decks of empty barges. The barge's caretaker was notorious for letting people use it for a few francs."

Henri frowned. "Let me guess. This happened thirty years ago."

Ali looked at him, astonished. "How did you know that?"

"Thirty years ago, a lot was going on," Henri answered.

"What are you going to do now?" Ava asked Henri.

"I have to go to the mansion. They're fitting me with a harness and showing me what I need to do on the roof so I don't kill myself tomorrow night."

"Henri!" Ava gasped.

"Don't worry, Ava. I have no intention of dying," Henri replied. "I'll leave that to others."

Somehow, Henri's words didn't reassure her.

CHAPTER 20

Leaving the café, Ava was in shock. It was almost impossible to wrap her mind around the fact that a couple had died on the same barge that the jewel thief had died on.

A coincidence?

Ava would be a fool to believe that. The film, the barge, the mansion... everything was part of an intricate plot. While Ava had no idea what the plot was, she was convinced that it was about more than finding the Tiger Emerald.

When she reached the key shop on the rue Mazarine, she was the only customer. In minutes, she obtained two copies of the keys to the mansion... one set for her and one set for Henri.

With time to spare before she went to the production office,

Ava headed to a café on the nearby rue de Buci -- the same café where she had eaten lunch with Martin the day before.

After checking its terrace and interior to see if the irascible screenwriter was there, Ava sat down at an outdoor table in the sun. She closed her eyes and soaked in its glorious rays.

Sometimes, life was so simple… a ray of sunshine, a good glass of wine and problems vanished.

"A croque madame and a glass of white wine?"

Startled, Ava opened her eyes. A waiter was hovering over her. It was the same waiter from the day before.

"You remember what I ordered?" Ava asked, curious.

The waiter shrugged. "That goes with the territory."

"Has my friend been here today?" Ava asked.

The waiter nodded. "He had a coffee and a croissant over an hour ago. He sat outside reading the newspaper. He got really upset when he read about the American star who was robbed. He was so upset he started shaking. I told him that it made no sense getting upset over things that don't concern us. Stolen jewels don't have anything to do with most people's lives."

But a stolen jewel might have something to do with Martin's life, Ava thought. The article she had read at Café Zola had mentioned the jewel thief's death. Was that what had disturbed Martin?

The waiter pointed at the table she and Martin had eaten at yesterday and cracked a smile. "I'm saving his table for him. Today is croque monsieur number four. I promised him that when he reached ten, it would be on the house."

Puzzled, Ava frowned. "Four? He comes here twice a day?"

The waiter ticked off the sandwiches on his fingers. "Wednesday, Thursday, Friday and today. That makes four."

Ava couldn't believe what she was hearing. Martin had arrived the same day that the man was killed on the barge. Why hadn't he called the production company when he arrived?

The answer was obvious.

He didn't want them to know what he was up to.

Immediately, Ava was on her feet. "I have to go. I'll be back later." She almost knocked the waiter over in her haste to leave.

When she reached the Cour de Rohan, she typed in the code, crossed the cobblestone courtyard and entered Martin's building. This time, she took the elevator. When she reached the top floor, she knocked on his door. When no one answered, she leaned out the hallway window and peered into his apartment. There was no sign of anyone.

Nothing ventured, nothing gained.

Ava took the keys to his apartment out of her pocket, unlocked the door and stepped inside.

"Martin? Are you here? It's Ava!"

There was no response. The apartment was silent.

After a rapid look around, Ava walked over his laptop on a table and opened it. She hit a key. The laptop lit up. It asked for the code. Frustrated, she closed it.

She eyed the living room looking for a clue. There was nothing she could see.

She moved to the bedroom door and opened it. The bed was made. Everything was very neat. Terrified that Martin would return and discover her, she forced herself to overcome her qualms about searching through his belongings. It was now or never.

First, she opened the closet. There was a row of pink checked shirts hanging there. Seeing his suitcase, she pulled it out. A luggage tag was on it. Just as the waiter had said, Martin had arrived four days ago on the 6 a.m. Eurostar from London. She ripped the luggage tag off and stuffed it in her pocket. As she put the suitcase back, something caught her eye. Silver reflective paint was on the toe of a sneaker next to the suitcase. She picked up both sneakers. Each one had streaks of metallic paint on their soles.

Ava felt sick. It resembled the paint the crew had used on the deck of the boat.

With rising panic, Ava put the sneakers back in place. She left the bedroom and closed the door behind her. In a hurry to leave, she checked the kitchen and the living room one last time. Noticing a trashcan under the table, she pulled it out. There was an empty package of tobacco and a paper that had been crushed into a ball. Ava removed the paper and smoothed it out. Stunned, she read the words written on it: You know who did it.

It was the same writing as the note in the production office.

Had Martin written it?

Unable to breathe, Ava crushed the paper into a ball and put it back in the trashcan.

She had to leave while she still could. Dashing out of the apartment, she locked the door behind her and ran down the steps. When she reached the ground floor, she hurried out of the building The moment her feet hit the cobblestones in the courtyard, she began to run. She stopped only when she turned onto the rue Saint-André-des-Arts.

Seeing the café across from the building that Madame LeGris had gone into yesterday, Ava entered it and sat down at a window table. She needed to calm down before she went to the production office.

"What can I get you if anything?"

Ava looked up. It was the same waiter she had run out on the day before. "A chausson aux pommes and an espresso. No, make that a double espresso."

The waiter nodded and left.

Leaning forward, Ava checked the street. If Martin came down it on his way to the set, she would see him. If Madame LeGris reappeared, she would also see her.

Ava sat back in her chair and examined what she had just learned.

What did Martin's secret arrival in Paris, his reaction to the newspaper, the silver paint on his shoes and the note in the trash mean?

Had Martin killed the jewel thief? Was that why he had seemed so carefree at lunch? Even if he hadn't killed him, Martin had obviously been at the barge. If not, where had the reflective paint on his sneakers come from? Had he written the note or had he received it? Ava had so many questions and so few answers.

"A double espresso and a chausson aux pommes," the waiter said, setting her order before her.

Ava bit into the chausson aux pommes. It was overly sweet with a touch of cinnamon. Reenergized from the sugar rush, Ava began to organize her thoughts.

Martin was in Paris the day of the death and had hidden that from her. The paint meant that he had gone to the barge. However, if Martin had killed the jewel thief, he would have known that the shoot would be postponed. Yet, he had seemed genuinely surprised.

On the other hand, if he had killed the thief, it would have been in his interest to act surprised. Why hadn't Martin asked her why the shoot on the barge had been canceled? Was that because he knew the answer? If he knew the answer, then why had he been so upset to learn about the mansion?

As Ava sipped her espresso, she wondered if Martin had been the one who pushed Simon. Nate had said that Martin hadn't answered his phone. There could be a million reasons for that.

As much as Ava had come to like Martin, he clearly knew more than he pretended to know. Right Martin or wrong Martin, the screenwriter was up to his neck in whatever was going on. She had to discover just what that it was before there was a fourth death.

CHAPTER 21

When Ava entered the production office, two crew members were working in the corner. There was no sign of Jaspar, Lance, or Nate. She guessed that they were at the set with the rest of the crew.

After a quick glance around, Ava entered the producers' office, slipped the mansion keys onto the rack and hurried back into the main office.

"I told you to come after lunch," Nate said as he came through the front door. He looked tired and tense.

Ava smiled. "I couldn't wait to see how Martin ended the film. Did he send the last pages?"

Nate's expression darkened. He shifted from one foot to the other, frowning.

"He didn't send them?" Ava asked, puzzled by Nate's reaction.

"That might have been better," Nate replied. "Let's go into the office."

Ava followed him inside. Nate took a few sheets of paper off his desk and handed them to her.

"Go ahead. Read them. I want your opinion."

Ava leaned against the edge of Jaspar's desk and began to read.

INT. NIGHT -- NEIGHBORHOOD BAR

Angel, Ken and Marty are seated at a table in the corner of a tiny bar. All three are tense.

Behind the bar, the bartender is chatting to the only other client -- a tall, dark-haired man in his late twenties.

At the table, an angry Marty speaks to Ken. "You said the money was for the film. That's the only reason I helped you."

Ken glares at him with contempt. "It is for the film."

Marty clenches his fists. "Then why didn't you pay the crew?"

A look of furor flashes across Ken's face. "You should thank me for getting your film made. I believed in you when no one did."

As if slapped, Marty backs down. Ken reaches out and puts his hand on

Angel's hand.

Angel pulls her hand away and speaks to Ken. "When are we meeting the fence?

Ken checks his watch. "In thirty minutes on the barge."

Marty leans forward. "Are you bringing the emerald with you?"

Ken eyes him, incredulous. "I'm not stupid. When I see the color of his money, I'll send Angel back to get it."

Marty presses him. "Where did you hide it?"

Ken shakes his head. "Why would I tell you that?"

Angel looks at Marty. "We'll finish the film. I promise. After Ken takes his share, we'll have ours. It's for the film."

Moved, Marty smiles at Angel. His eyes tear up. "Thanks. That means a lot to me."

Seeing how Marty looks at Angel, Ken puts his arm around her shoulder and kisses her on the side of her head. "You're my angel, aren't you? You'll always be my angel. No one can break the bond between us."

Angel moves away from him. "That's enough, Ken!"

Suddenly impatient, Ken stands up. "Angel? Shall we go?"

Reluctantly, she rises to her feet and follows him out of the bar.

Three other crew members arrive and join Marty. Marty orders a round of drinks for everyone.

As Ken and Angel leave, the man at the bar stands up and follows them out.

Ellipse.

EXT. NIGHT -- RIVER/BARGE

The barge explodes.

Voiceover: Ken and Angel were never seen again nor was the jewel. Who betrayed them? Who gave away their secrets?

Fade to Black.

White-faced, Ava put the pages down. "What does this mean? Did Martin drop them off?"

Nate's face clouded over. "A courier service delivered them. I don't know what it means except it isn't good."

"What was Lance's reaction?" Ava asked, worried.

"He read the pages, turned white and left without a word. Jaspar and I agreed not to show them to Simon. It would only make things worse."

"What does Jaspar think?" Ava asked.

"He doesn't know what to think," Nate said. "He wonders if it's true, or if it's a figment of Martin's imagination."

Ava was silent. Now was the time to tell Nate what she had learned about the deaths on the barge and Martin. She decided against it. She wasn't sure she could trust him. "What are you going to do now?"

"Make the film," Nate replied.

Ava narrowed her eyes. "Have you spoken with Martin today?"

Nate shook his head. "We called his cell phone. He doesn't answer. We even had the concierge go up and knock on his door. No one answered."

"Do you have any idea who Angel is? Marty must be Martin. Ken was the director on his film. Could the three of them have carried out a jewel heist?"

"It would appear so… if Angel exists," Nate said. "To me, these pages sound like Martin went on a bender and spit out everything in his imagination. I suspect that Angel was the character in his film who killed herself."

"And if she was real and died in an explosion on the barge with Ken?" Ava asked.

Nate shook his head. "If she died in an explosion on a barge, the police would have known about it. Ken had a family and friends. People don't vanish like that, today or thirty years ago. My theory is that Martin learned about the death on our barge. He got drunk, and the past and present got muddled up in his mind."

"What if it's true? What if Martin did steal a jewel?" Ava asked.

"Martin? A jewel thief? That would be an odd twist," Nate said as he crooked his head sideways. "Ava, my job is to get the film made. I intend to do that. I'm not going to run around playing detective."

"What if it's about the Tiger Emerald?" Ava insisted. "What if it really is missing, and people are looking for it."

"Then I hope they find it. I don't care as long as their search doesn't interfere with shooting. Let me be clear... I don't like puzzles, and I don't like what's going on. If I see Martin, I'll wring his neck. He was hired to write a script not to give in to flights of fancy," Nate said, furious.

Ava crossed her arms. "Aren't you curious as to why someone financed the film?"

Nate shook his head. "I'm not curious. I'm incredulous. But if you look at many of the films that get made, *Death on the Quai* isn't the worst script in the world."

"It's close," Ava replied.

Nate burst out laughing. "I promise you that if I see anything nefarious going on, I'll let you know. Until then, we have a lot of work to do. As tomorrow is a night shoot and our first day of principal photography, we're knocking off early today. They'll be drinks and food at a nearby bar."

"Is the crew up to a party?" Ava asked, astonished.

"A crew is always up to a party. Don't forget, they don't know what we know. For them, it's a film shoot like any other," Nate said.

"And the dead jewel thief on the barge?" Ava asked. "They know about him!"

"The police said it was an accident."

Seeing that she didn't agree with him, Nate reached out and touched her shoulder. A shiver ran through her.

"Ava, sometimes a dead jewel thief is just a dead jewel thief."

"And sometimes, he's not," Ava replied, unswayed by Nate's words.

CHAPTER 22

The crew was streaming into the production office. It was time to close shop for the day.

"I thought you'd gone AWOL," Jaspar said as he appeared behind Ava who was working in a corner of the office.

On the phone, Ava put her finger to her lips. After she finished the call, she hung up and turned to him. "If I weren't here, who would solve all these problems?" She waved her hand at the table in front of her that was covered with post-its and scribbled notes, the fruits of her effort.

"You haven't lost your efficiency," Jaspar said in mock admiration.

"Has Martin appeared?" Ava asked.

"There's no sign of him. He's not answering his phone, but that's not surprising. Did you read his ending?"

Ava nodded. "What if it's true? What if Ken and Angel are dead?"

"If Martin's Ken was Ken Waters, the director, someone would have noticed that he went missing. He was working on a film. Even thirty years ago, people didn't vanish like that. As for Angel, we don't know if she exists outside of Martin's mind," Jaspar said with a heavy sigh. "Nate believes that Martin went on a bender and mixed things up. Alcohol does that."

"Alcohol can also act as a truth serum," Ava replied.

Jaspar didn't look convinced. "When Martin arrives, we'll ask him. It's best he stays away from the set. Simon actually worked today. Henri has a positive influence on him. For the first time, I believe that we'll make the film. My only worry is Lance. Since he read Martin's ending, he's fallen completely apart."

Ava looked puzzled. "After all that's happened, why is he taking it so hard?"

"Lance is a worrier. Where someone else sees a problem that can be solved, he sees a catastrophe that is about to sweep him away."

Ava found herself siding with Lance. Something major was about to happen. Jaspar and Nate should be more worried that they appeared to be. *Maybe Jaspar wanted people to stay calm until he had the jewel...* Immediately, Ava felt disloyal. She was assuming that Jaspar was after the jewel.

"Let's go to the party," Jaspar said. "I've had enough."

"Jaspar, I have a question for you," Ava blurted out.

Seeing the grave expression on her face, Jaspar stared at her. "Why so serious?"

"Because it's a serious question."

Jaspar crossed his arms. "I'm waiting."

"Why were you at the mansion late last night?"

Jaspar stepped back, bewildered. "No. Why do you ask?"

"Because I saw you," Ava stated as she fixed her eyes on him.

"What were you doing at the mansion?" Jaspar asked, astonished.

"I left my keys there," Ava replied, surprised at how easy lying had become. She had lied to both Henri and Jaspar today, and the day wasn't even over.

"What exactly did you see?" Jaspar asked.

"It was pitch black, but I saw you. You were running your hands around the molding around the fireplace."

Jaspar looked away. "I didn't think anyone else was there. What did you see then?"

"After you went into the countess's dressing room, I heard footsteps in the reception room."

Jaspar listened with a strange expression on his face. "Did you see the person?"

"No. It was too dark. Then someone pushed me in the closet. I was so frightened I stayed there for a long time," Ava admitted.

Alarm spread across Jaspar's face. "Any idea who pushed you?"

Ava shook her head.

Jaspar took her hands in his. "Promise me you won't go to the mansion alone again. It's dangerous."

"What were you doing there?" Ava asked.

Before Jaspar could answer, Nate strode over to them. He looked from Ava to Jaspar and at their clasped hands. "Sorry to interrupt. The producer usually makes a toast to the film at the beginning of the party, and since Lance has disappeared, it's up to you, Jaspar."

Jaspar released Ava's hands. "Duty calls."

Ava watched him walk away with Nate. He hadn't answered her question. Oddly, she hadn't liked that Nate had seen Jaspar holding her hand. She wondered what that meant.

The party was in a small bar on a side street off rue Saint-André-des-Arts. The bar was packed when Ava arrived. Everyone was in good spirits. Jaspar had finished his speech and was laughing and chatting with Simon. There was no sign of Lance or Martin. Henri had texted Ava to ask that she meet him at 10 p.m. on the quay near the production office. Ava took a glass of white wine and looked around. Most of the people she had seen before. Nate was talking with a woman. Ava could only see her back.

Noticing Ava, Nate waved her over. "I have a surprise for you."

Frowning, Ava joined him. The woman turned. It was Loulou Pleyel, the location scout.

Loulou was astonished to see Ava. "What are you doing here?"

"I'm working on the film," Ava replied with a quick grin, delighted to see Loulou. "What are you doing here?"

"I never say no to a party," Loulou joked. "I wanted to say goodbye to the crew before I start my next film. I'm off to the south of France tomorrow."

"No roofs?" Ava asked.

"No roofs, no tunnels, not even a tower…" Loulou replied.

Ava took a sip of her wine and raised her eyebrows. "This is fabulous! How can the production afford this?"

"Madame LeGris generously provided the wine," Nate replied.

"The production is lucky she's so interested in the film," Loulou said.

Ava was puzzled. "Interested? What do you mean?"

"Lance told me he gives her a rundown of the production each day. She asks him lots of questions."

Ava was silent. Something about Loulou's answer troubled her.

"Maybe she thinks Lance needs encouragement," Loulou said. She lowered her voice. "He does."

"Did you visit any tunnels in this neighborhood for your last film?" Nate asked casually.

Ava jerked her head toward Nate. *Why was he asking that?*

Loulou nodded. "Beginning 800 years ago, the ground under this area was mined for stone. The miners would build narrow tunnels. Most have collapsed. Some became catacombs. The Germans connected some of them when they occupied Paris. We weren't able to visit them because they're too dangerous, but they still exist."

"The Germans built a platform on the roof of the LeGris mansion," Ava said. "You have an amazing view from there."

"I saw it. If you're not afraid of heights, you could walk over the roofs from the LeGris mansion to the set," Loulou said with real enthusiasm.

Nate shook his head. "Let's hope no one tries that! We have enough problems as it is."

The wardrobe woman who had dressed Henri the day before waved at Loulou from the other side of the room. "Loulou!" she shouted.

"My fans await me," Loulou said with a wide grin and walked off.

With a glass of wine in his hand, Jaspar joined Ava and Nate. "And a good time was had by all!" Jaspar said, raising his glass in the air.

"We have a tough shoot ahead of us. We'll need it," Nate replied, sipping his wine.

Jaspar eyed the room. "Lance?"

Nate shook his head. "No. It's still early. He might come later."

Jaspar's phone beeped. It was a text message. He looked at it. A strange look came over his face as he read it.

Ava stared at Jaspar with a probing look. "Anything important?"

Jaspar shook his head. "Nothing I can't deal with." He smiled at Ava and Nate. "I'd better circulate and play the producer."

Ava wondered what the message said. Knowing Jaspar as she did, she could tell he was lying. The message had startled him. Eyeing Nate, she could tell that he was thinking the same thing.

"More wine?" Nate asked.

Ava handed him her glass. "I'd be a fool to say no."

Leaving the party in full swing, Ava hurried from the bar to the quay where she was to meet Henri. She was anxious to tell him all she had learned. Overhead, the weather had changed. The wind was blowing and the sky was dark.

If this were a film, something bad would be about to happen, Ava thought looking up at the menacing sky.

She turned onto the street the countess's mansion was on and continued toward the Seine. As she strode past the small triangular bar, she saw the faintest flicker of a light inside. Slowing, she went up to the window and peered in. The red velvet curtain blocked her view of the interior, but a sliver of light was visible between the end of the curtain and the wall.

Someone was there.

Instinctively, Ava walked up to the door and turned the handle. When it opened, she stepped inside and went through the red velvet curtain. Immediately, someone grabbed her and put their hand over her mouth.

"You shouldn't have come here!"

CHAPTER 23

Ava struggled with the person who was holding her. Unable to free herself, she kicked back hard.

"Ow!" Lance said, releasing Ava. He bent over to rub his shin.

"What do you think you're doing?" Ava asked.

In response, Lance's eyes darted to the red velvet curtain. "I have to lock the door!" He dashed through the curtain. Seconds later, he was back.

"How did you know I was here?" Lance asked, shifting nervously from foot to foot.

Ava walked to the edge of the curtain and pulled it tight to the wall. "I saw light." Turning, she saw that Lance was in even worse shape than when he learned about the dead body on the barge. His eyes were bulging out of his head and he was sweating.

"What are you doing here? How did you get in?" Ava asked.

Lance held up a key. "I found the key to the bar with the master key set to the mansion. The bar belongs to the mansion. I imagine it used to be for the guardian."

"Why are you here?" Ava asked.

"When I read Martin's ending, it all became clear. The jewel is hidden in the mansion," Lance said. "I saw lights in the mansion last night. I figured there must be a secret way in. I thought of the bar."

"Have you found the secret passage?" Ava asked.

"I didn't have time," Lance said, throwing a reproachful look at Ava. "You arrived."

Ava pulled out her phone to text Henri when she heard the sound of a key in the lock. "Turn out the light!" she hissed to Lance.

Lance hit the light switch. The bar went dark. Ava grabbed his arm and pulled him into a small area behind the bar covered with a curtain. She could feel Lance's heart beating a mile a minute. She prayed he wouldn't make any noise.

A few seconds later, someone walked past the area where Ava and Lance were hidden. Whoever it was didn't turn the light on. That indicated that they knew where they were going. There was the sound of something heavy hitting the ground. Then everything went silent.

Sensing that Lance was about to speak, Ava put her finger over his lips. They stood in the dark there for what seemed like an eternity. Then Ava opened the curtain a crack and peered out. Seeing no one, she inched forward and turned her phone's flashlight on. The bar was empty.

"Is anyone there?" Lance asked.

Ava shone the light on his face. "No."

She stepped out and waited. Whoever had been there was gone. She turned the light on. Lance pointed to the back corner.

"Look! The trap door to the cellar is open."

Ava walked over to it and pointed her flashlight down into the dark space below. A narrow wooden ladder attached to the wall led down to it.

"This must be how the ghost got in," Lance said.

"Whoever just went down there was not a ghost," Ava replied with a frown. Taking a deep breath, she grabbed the wooden ladder. "Follow me."

Lance winced. "Into the cellar?"

Ava didn't answer him. She was already on her way down. The wooden ladder had rotted through in places. It was slimy to the touch. Ava was glad she couldn't see anything as she was sure she'd be horrified by what she was touching. When she reached the bottom, she shone her flashlight up so Lance could climb down. When he reached the tiny, dank cellar, he took in his surroundings, terrified.

"This isn't a good idea!" Lance warned.

Ava ignored him and shone her flashlight around the cellar. Humidity was dripping down its walls. Turning, she saw a small opening in the wall. She walked over to it and peered inside. It was a tunnel. It was too dark to see down it.

Lance joined her and touched the tunnel's damp walls. "We're right near the Seine. I wouldn't be surprised if this floods when the river is high."

"Follow me. Whatever you do, don't speak," Ava said to Lance as she plunged into the tunnel. Its walls were made of stone. They had collapsed in several places. Ava climbed over the stones on the ground and crept forward. She regretted not calling Henri from the bar. If the tunnel collapsed, he would never know that she was down there. Lance followed Ava. After a few hundred feet, Ava calculated that they must be under the mansion.

"Ava! Look!" Lance said, pointing at a stone staircase built into the wall on their left.

Ava eyed the staircase.

"Do you think Ken is dead?" Lance asked.

"We don't even know if he exists," Ava replied, trying to calm Lance's growing hysteria.

Lance shook his head. "Of course, he exists. That's what this is about… and the jewel, of course."

Ava stared at Lance. *Why was he fixated on Ken? Did he know something about the director's death?*

They started up the steep stone stairs. When they reached the top, there was a thick wooden door that was open. They went through it. They were in a narrow space. A wooden wall was in front of them. A wooden panel in the bottom of the wall was partly open. Ava crouched down and pushed on it. It gave onto a narrow space. As Ava crawled through the opening, she smelled violets. They must be in the countess's wardrobe.

Behind her, Lance was shaking so hard that Ava thought he'd faint. She turned her flashlight and phone off.

"Turn off your phone!" Ava ordered Lance.

He fumbled in his pocket, took his phone out and turned it off.

"No matter what happens, no talking!" Ava whispered as she opened the closet door and stepped out into the dressing room. Followed by Lance, she crept through the dark room. Cautiously, she pushed the door to the sitting room open and entered it. The door to the reception hall was ajar. It was brightly lit with film lights. The Venetian chandeliers with colored Murano glass had been taken down and were in boxes in a corner of the room, wrapped in protective bubble wrap.

Was the production doing last minute lighting tests? Ava wondered.

Peering through the door, Ava watched Simon arrive. He moved to a chair and sat down. Ava wondered what he was doing.

Seconds later, she had her answer.

Martin entered the room. He was astonished to see Simon. "What are you doing here?"

Simon held up his phone. "I'm here for the same reason you are. I received a message."

Both men turned when they heard footsteps coming up the steps.

Jaspar appeared at the door. He nodded to both men. "Are we the only ones?"

"So far," Simon said. He read the message off his phone. "It's time to discover what is going on. 10:15 at the mansion."

"I got the same message," Martin said.

Hearing footsteps, the trio turned. Nate entered the room followed by Henri. Nate held up his phone. "I hope we're not late."

Suddenly, the lights went out and a screen came down from

the ceiling. A film began to play. It was an old film that had been shot on a handheld camera. It showed people at a party in the countess's garden. There was no sound.

From her hiding spot, Ava recognized the countess. A tall man in his early forties with dark hair that fell across his face walked up and kissed her. He put his hand around the countess's shoulder.

A shiver went up Ava's spine. The man must be Ken.

A young woman in her twenties with blond hair appeared. She was chatting with a man in his late twenties. When the man turned, Ava recognized him. It was a younger Martin. Other people walked onto the screen, drinking and laughing. A wimpy young man in his early twenties joined the group. The man wore thick glasses. Everyone ignored him.

"It's Gofer!" Martin said out loud in astonishment. "I forgot he even existed."

The film continued for a few more minutes with more shots of the party. Then the screen went dark, and the lights went on.

A woman entered the reception room from the hallway. Ava recognized the woman as an older version of the blond woman in the film. She was also the same woman who had left the building Madame LeGris had entered.

Seeing her, Martin began to shake. "Angel! I thought you were dead."

Next to Ava, Lance gasped and moved to enter the reception room. Ava gripped his arm and held him back.

"I'm glad you're all here," Angel said, smiling at everyone.

Henri spoke to the woman. "Let me introduce myself. Henri DeAth. I wasn't invited."

"I saw him in the street and brought him along," Nate explained.

Angel smiled. "I have no objection to his presence."

Simon glared at her. "Can you tell us what this is all about?"

"Didn't you receive the end of the script?" Angel asked.

Nate's eyes lit up. "You wrote it?"

"I wrote it," Angel said with a nod. She turned to Simon. "To answer your question, this is about discovering who killed Ken thirty years ago and almost killed me."

Henri raised his eyebrows. "And the Tiger Emerald?"

"You mean finding it?" Angel asked.

Henri nodded. "Do you know where it is?"

Angel smiled. "I have a good idea. But that's not why we're here. For those of you who didn't see my ending, I'll read it to you," Angel held the script pages up and began to read. When she reached the voiceover at the end: *Ken and Angel were never seen again nor was the jewel. Who betrayed them? Who gave away their secrets?"* she asked as her voice cracked with emotion.

"I betrayed you. I gave away your secrets," Martin announced dramatically. "I was jealous. I was drunk. I remember telling some of the crew that you and Ken were getting money to complete the film."

Angel whirled toward him. "Who was there?"

"I don't remember," Martin whimpered. "I only remember that I hated Ken and wanted him to suffer. I didn't want him to die. I never would have hurt you."

Angel eyed Simon. "Do you have any idea what happened?"

Simon shrugged. "Perhaps my cousin was involved. Maybe that's why he decided to become a vicar... to redeem his sins. I can't tell you that."

"Why now? Why did you decide to carry out this scheme today and not earlier?" Nate asked Angel.

"I had to wait until my husband died," Angel replied.

Astonished, everyone stared at her.

Henri caught his breath. "You're Madame LeGris?"

Angel nodded. "I'm Madame LeGris."

Confused, Jaspar shook his head. "You're too young to be her. The woman I saw with Lance was older."

"You never saw my face. You just assumed I was older as my husband was almost ninety when he died."

"Did Lance know about this?" Jaspar asked.

"No. He didn't know about my plan," Angel said.

"Why did you choose my production company?" Jaspar asked.

"I had my reasons," Angel replied and fell silent.

Henri stepped forward. "What happened after you left the bar?"

"Ken and I met the man who was going to buy the emerald. They discussed the price and agreed to meet later that night. When the man left, Ken told me to go home. He said he'd deal with everything. I offered to get the jewel and bring it back. He laughed in my face and refused to tell me where he had hidden it. I knew it was in the countess's mansion, but I didn't know where. I was angry. I left. Back home, I became angrier and angrier. I decided to go back to the barge and confront him. I was sure he was going to take all the money and leave us with nothing. When I reached the quay, the fire department was there as well as the river patrol. Later the police found two bodies. I fled back here to the countess's mansion. She was in Rome. As I was working on the production, I had the keys. I hid here. Someone came to the mansion that night.

I was afraid they knew I was alive. I went over the roofs and slipped through the rooftop entrance into the LeGris mansion. That's how I met Louis LeGris."

"Who was the woman with Ken?" Henri asked.

Angel shook her head. "I don't know. Despite what everyone thought, I wasn't Ken's girlfriend. He was my father. He'd had a one night stand with my mother. I was the result of that night of passion. He'd never acknowledged me as his child. I wanted to meet him. I came to Paris and got a job on the film. When he made moves on me, I told him who I was. He said he was too young to have a daughter my age. He pretended that he and I were having a fling. I'm not sorry he's dead. He was a horrible person and intended to keep the money from the beginning."

"You have no idea who the woman was?" Nate asked.

Martin's features tensed. "At that time, there were a lot of people sleeping rough on the quay. I imagine she was one who caught his eye."

Jaspar eyed Martin. "You stole the jewel?"

Martin nodded. "It wasn't difficult. The countess often left the jewel around. I'm surprised someone didn't take it earlier."

"Why didn't anyone miss Ken?" Henri asked with a puzzled look on his face.

"Because he wrote the crew from Brazil," Angel replied.

"But he was dead," Jaspar protested.

"No one knew that. My late husband thought of everything," Angel said. "My husband fell in love with me from the moment he found me hiding in his mansion. I don't know why. I tried to be the wife he wanted. We were happy. I promised him that I would leave sleeping dogs lie. But now he's dead. I need to understand what happened."

"Did he keep the jewel?" Henri asked.

Angel was astonished. "Keep it? He bought it!"

"I don't understand," Nate said as he paced back and forth. "You said you didn't know where Ken had hidden it."

"We didn't know. We only knew that the emerald was hidden somewhere in the mansion. My husband went to the countess and told her what had happened. When she learned that Ken had stolen it and had died, she wanted nothing more to do with the Tiger Emerald. She sold it to my husband for a very fair price. We also bought her mansion."

"Where is the emerald?" Jaspar asked.

"Wherever Ken hid it. He said that it was safe and no one would find it,' Angel said.

"You left a valuable jewel in the mansion all these years?" Nate asked, incredulous.

"We didn't know where it was. My husband was very wealthy. Hidden here or in a vault, what's the difference?" Angel asked.

Henri crossed his arms. "What about the jewel thief, George Maurel? He's dead. Did you have anything to do with that?"

Angel nodded. "He sent me a letter. I went to see him…"

Suddenly, Lance burst out of the sitting room. "Don't say anything else, aunt." Lance turned to everyone. "I killed the man on the barge. He threatened me. I pushed him. He fell and died. I didn't mean to do it."

"What time was that?" Angel asked.

Lance's eyes darted around the room feverishly. "I don't remember exactly. Maybe 9. No! It was 9:30."

Angel shook her head. "Thank you for trying to protect me, Lance. But I didn't kill George Maurel. I saw him at 9:45. He threatened to reveal that my husband had the jewel. I told him he could reveal whatever he wanted because he was wrong. George Maurel was alive when I left."

Martin paced back and forth. "I saw him at 10:30. He told me that we should work together to find the jewel." Martin turned to Angel. "He said you were living in Brazil. He had no idea you were Madame LeGris. I was so happy to learn that you were alive that I agreed to help him. Afterward, I began to think that he'd lied to me, and you were dead. I was devastated. That's why I was so surprised to see you tonight. Surprised, but happy." Tears began to roll down Martin's face.

"What happened at the barge?" Jaspar asked.

Everyone was silent.

"We'll never know," Angel said with a sigh. "I had hoped it would be like in a detective novel. I'd bring you all here, and one of you would confess. But Simon is the wrong Simon, and things don't happen in real life like they do in books."

"Who is the man who left the bar? The tall stranger," Jaspar asked in a strangled voice.

"A journalist," Angel responded. "He was working on a story about jewel thefts. Maybe he'd learned about the Tiger Emerald and intended to write about it. He never did. I always wondered why he protected me. It would have been a big scoop to turn me in, especially after I became Madame LeGris."

Hidden in the sitting room, Ava realized that the journalist was Jaspar's father. She wondered if he was responsible for the deaths on the barge.

Lance was confused. "Then we'll never know who caused the explosion on the barge?"

"I'm afraid not," Angel said.

"And the jewel?" Simon asked.

Angel shrugged. "I never want to see it again. Whoever finds it can keep it. But remember it's cursed. The countess's father and Ken died because of it."

"What are we going to do now?" Lance asked, looking around.

"Sleep!" Simon replied in a firm voice. "We shoot tomorrow."

Martin raised his eyebrows. "I need to get the end of the script done. Not that your end is bad, Angel... but mine will be better."

Angel smiled at him. "I don't doubt that, Martin. You always had a wonderful imagination."

Everyone began to leave. When Henri reached the door, he glanced back toward the sitting room where Ava was hiding. He stared at it, then turned and followed the others out.

CHAPTER 24

Hidden in the sitting room, Ava waited for what was about to happen. She had no doubts that something momentous was about to take place. Every bone in her body told her that. When Angel had announced that the Tiger Emerald was hidden in the mansion, she was baiting someone to come and find it. Ava guessed that the person who appeared might be the person who had killed George Maurel, the jewel thief.

As the minutes ticked by, Ava heard a movement at the far end of the sitting room. Turning she saw Jaspar emerge from behind the drapes.

"Jaspar? How did you get in here?" Ava whispered.

Jaspar put his finger to his lips and moved toward her. When he was next to her, he lit a match. Ava stepped back in astonishment. The man wasn't Jaspar. While he looked like Jaspar, he was older and taller.

Ava ran her eyes over the man, unable to get over his resemblance with his son. "Graham Porter?"

"In the flesh!" Graham said with a worried look in his eyes. "Whoever killed Ken will soon be here for the jewel. We need to be ready."

Ava was stunned. "You know the identity of Ken's killer?"

Graham nodded. "I have a good idea who it is. I just need to confirm it."

Before Ava could ask him more questions, there was a sound of someone moving through the reception hall. Graham put his finger to his lips and blew out the match. Hidden behind the door, Ava watched a flashlight bounce off the reception hall walls. The man carrying the flashlight headed directly to the Venetian chandeliers made of colored Murano glass that were boxed up in the corner and began to shine the light down on them.

As Graham and Ava watched, the man tipped the box over and the chandeliers crashed to the ground. He crouched down next to them and ran his flashlight over the glass ornaments. He pulled some off and examined them, before discarding them and continuing his search. Every now and then, he'd pull off one and step on it, crushing it. After repeating this process several times, he stepped on one that didn't break. He reached down and picked it up. He shone his light at it and headed to the door.

Before he could reach the door, the lights went on. Henri, Nate and Angel were standing there staring at Simon who had the emerald in his hand.

"Get out of my way," Simon ordered as his ears turned bright red.

"You should have stayed away," Graham said, stepping from the sitting room.

Suddenly, there was a loud noise from the dressing room. Lance, Jaspar and Martin came bursting out from it and ran into the reception room. Stunned, they stopped when they saw everyone.

Martin reeled back. "Is this a party we weren't invited to?"

Jaspar went white when he saw his father. "Dad?!"

Ava followed them into the reception hall and looked at the jewel in Simon's hand. The Tiger Emerald existed, and people had died for it.

Unafraid, Angel walked up toward Simon. "The jewel is yours. I was serious when I said that. In exchange, I want to know what happened on the barge with Ken. The statute of limitations is up. What you tell us will stay within these walls."

Simon eyed the jewel in his hand. "That sounds fair. I didn't cause the explosion, but I didn't stop it either."

All at once, Martin realized who Simon really was. "Gofer? You were behind it? That's impossible."

"You all thought I was stupid. Even my cousin treated me as a non-entity. When I learned about the jewel, I decided to act," Simon snarled.

Stricken, Martin put his hand to his throat. "It's all my fault."

Simon looked at him in disgust. "Stop whining. I didn't need you to tell me. I found out on my own. Everyone treated me as if I was invisible. Being invisible meant I learned a lot."

Angel kept her eyes on Simon. "What happened on the barge?"

Simon smiled. "I waited until you and the man had left. I thought Ken had the money already. I went on the barge and told him I wanted it. He mocked me and refused. The woman he was with was cooking in the kitchen. Her pan caught on fire. When he ran to help her, the flames spread. The fire trapped them. Ken screamed for help. I left, locking the door behind me."

"You let him die!" Nate accused.

"I let him die," Simon confirmed. "If I had tried to help them, I might have died. That was out of the question."

"Why did you accept the film?" Henri asked.

Simon roared in laughter. "I knew it was about the jewel. I

came back to get the emerald or at least try. In a way, I should thank Ken. His death freed me..."

"How?" Graham asked as he edged toward Simon.

"Before his death, people looked through me as if I didn't exist. That changed after Ken's death. It was as if I had a new power," Simon explained. "I got what I wanted."

"Did your cousin know about this?" Angel asked.

Simon smiled a self-contented smile. "Simon, the vicar! No. He had no idea what I was capable of."

"What about George Maurel?" Ava asked.

"I had nothing to do with his death. Someone here killed him," Simon said running his eyes across the room. "You can discuss that when I'm gone because I'm leaving." His ears flushed red again.

"You're lying!" Martin said. "Gofer's ears always flashed red when he was annoyed or angry. I should have recognized you immediately."

"But you didn't, did you? I'm not the same man," Simon said as he moved to the door.

Nate went to block Simon. Angel put her hand on Nate's arm. "Let him leave. He told me what I wanted to know. It was worth the price of the jewel."

Suddenly, Ava remembered something that had been bothering her. "You killed George Maurel! Claire, the Assistant Director, found your keys down near the barge on the day that his body was found. But you insisted that you hadn't even gone down there," Ava said.

Lance stared at Simon. "When I left the office on the night of the murder, you were the last one there. You locked the door when you left. If your keys were found on the quay, that meant that you went there that night."

Simon grabbed Ava and pulled a knife out of his pocket. "Let me leave, or I'll hurt her."

Infuriated, Ava kicked Simon. He let go of her and reeled back. Then he bounded to the door, knocking into Henri. When Nate tried to stop Simon, Simon punched him. Nate fell backward and hit his head on the railing as Simon vanished down the stairs.

In a bound, Ava was at Nate's side. "Are you OK?"

Lance began to run toward the stairs. Henri stopped him.

"One dead man on the film is enough," Henri said.

"Shouldn't we call the police?" Martin asked.

Henri shook his head. "It won't bring Ken or the woman back to life. Plus, there's no proof Simon killed the jewel thief. It might have been an accident."

"What are we going to do now?" Lance asked.

Nate stood up with Ava and Henri's help. "Martin is going to go home and finish the script. Lance had better get his storyboard out as we start shooting tomorrow night, and, as of now, we don't have a director."

A huge smile crossed Lance's face "I'm going to direct it?"

"Unless there's another Lance in the room, yes…" Jaspar said.

Angel stared at Graham. "Why didn't you write about me and the jewel?"

"Because you didn't deserve it. When I realized that you had married Louis LeGris, I was happy for you and sad for me."

Angel kept her eyes on Graham but remained silent.

"You knew that. I didn't have to tell you," Graham said as he walked over to Angel and took her hands in his.

"You hired me because of my father?" Jaspar asked.

Angel nodded.

"Who sent the email from my account asking me to shut down the production?" Jaspar asked.

Graham raised his hand. "I did. When George Maurel contacted me, I realized that situation was dangerous. I didn't want anything to happen to you."

"Who wrote the note in the office?" Ava asked, with a frown.

Nate smiled. "That was me. If something was going on, I wanted to know before we started shooting."

"Who sent the note to me?" Martin asked.

Nate shook his head. "It wasn't me."

"Guilty," Jaspar responded. "I began to suspect that the note had been intended for you. You were the most logical suspect. There was only one way to find out. I had to send you the note and see how you reacted."

Martin smiled. "The most logical suspect… that would make a great title for a film."

Ava frowned. "Who shoved me in the closet?"

Angel smiled. "I did. I didn't want you to get hurt."

Henri looked from one person to another. "I don't about anyone else. But as I have to run across rooftops tomorrow, I intend to go and get some sleep."

EPILOGUE

The sun was streaming into the opulent suite in the Ritz Hotel on the Place Vendôme. The sculpted woodwork, period furniture, and thick carpets in shades of pale green, rose, and beige were complimented by enormous vases of flowers in the same tones. A heavy perfume wafted from the vases.

Madame LeGris was seated on the low couch speaking with Nate. She was dressed simply in trousers and a silk shirt. She was wearing her necklace with the large glass pendant on it. Her blond hair was tucked behind her ears. Watching her from across the room, Ava was struck by her natural elegance. Madame LeGris had the *je ne sais quoi,* inexplicable beauty that French women often had.

Jaspar walked up to Ava. "You survived the film shoot."

Ava smiled. "Barely."

"It couldn't have been that bad," Jaspar joked.

"Worse," Ava said. "I'll be happy to get back to my stand."

"Ali and his brother are doing a booming business without you," Henri said as he joined them.

"Well, competition is about to come back," Ava replied with a grin.

A waiter rolled in a cart with a magnum of champagne and foie gras canapés and pushed it to the corner of the room.

Graham Porter arrived and eyed the champagne. "I see I've arrived at the right time," Graham said as he walked over to Madame LeGris and kissed her on the cheek. She looked into his eyes and smiled.

Lance was pacing back and forth in front of the window talking on the phone. Hanging up, he grinned. "That was the film editor, we should have a first edit in a month."

The waiter popped the cork on the champagne, poured it into glasses and served everyone.

Angel LeGris stood up. "A toast to *Death on the Quai*. May it be the first film of many!"

Lance raised his glass to his aunt. "To my aunt, without you, the film wouldn't have gotten made."

Angel smiled at Lance. "You and your team had the talent. I

just had the money. I'd like to thank all of you for taking part in my little experiment. I needed to know what happened years ago. Now that I know, I can move on."

Ava raised her eyebrows. "Wasn't giving up the Tiger Emerald a high price to pay?"

"The jewel is cursed," Lance reminded everyone. "Simon will pay the price for his actions."

"It just doesn't seem fair to me that Simon got away with murder and got the jewel," Ava said with a tinge of regret. "No one would want to see a film end like that."

Henri eyed Graham who nodded.

"Angel, It's time to tell them the truth," Graham said.

A silence fell over the room.

Angel LeGris stood up. "There's something you all need to know." As everyone watched, she took off her glass pendant necklace. She walked over to the fireplace and smashed the glass pendant against the marble fireplace. When it broke, she picked the pieces of glass off a green stone. She held it up in the air. "The Tiger Emerald!"

Nate was astonished. "Then Simon didn't get the Tiger Emerald?"

Angel shook her head. "I'm a LeGris. My late husband would

have risen from his grave if I'd given the emerald away. I discovered by accident where it was hidden. I had a copy made. I wore the real emerald every day. That way, I knew it was safe."

Lance frowned. "Then Simon isn't cursed?"

Graham shook his head. "He is cursed. He did all this and didn't get what he wanted. Imagine his surprise when he discovers the emerald is a fake."

"Won't he want revenge?" Nate asked.

Angel shook her head. "I recorded his confession about Ken's death. I sent it to him. I told him I would send it to the newspapers if he ever tried to contact any of us again."

Ava eyed Angel with admiration. She was one tough woman.

Jaspar turned to Ava. "Without your help and Henri's, who knows what would have happened..." He eyed Graham who was holding Angel's hand. "Having Lance in the family will take some getting used to."

Ava smiled at Jaspar. Working with him this last month had shown her that he was a good friend, but he lacked the spark that she wanted in a man she was seeing. What Jaspar was lacking was a sort of craziness. He was too normal. Or maybe she was too odd... Still, she was glad he was back in her life as a friend.

Henri joined them. "I can't wait to see my screen debut. If the critics say that Ian Granger is great, I'll know it's because of me. If they don't like his acting then it's his fault."

"Did you know that the emerald was a fake?" Ava asked Henri.

"I suspected it. Louis LeGris was hardly the type of man to leave an expensive jewel hidden on a chandelier," Henri responded.

"What was your aunt doing at the apartment on the rue Saint-André-des-Arts?" Ava asked Lance.

"She wanted to walk around normally. Being Madame LeGris wasn't always easy," Lance said. Looking at his aunt, he smiled. "Angel will take some getting used to."

Suddenly, Ava took out her phone. She scanned through her photos until she reached the photo of the mailboxes in the building on the rue Saint-André-des-Arts. She read through them. "Anne Gelina."

Lance nodded. "Gelina was her mother's married name."

Henri looked at Ava's phone. "You were right. The answer was the name on the mailbox."

Frustrated, Ava went to get a foie gras canapé. Nate joined her. "Are you ready?"

"For what?" Ava asked.

Nate smiled. "I thought I'd come and shoot in your tower… if that's OK…"

"But shooting is finished," Ava said.

"That's exactly why I waited. I didn't want to ask you out during the shoot," Nate said, sheepishly.

Ava hid a smile. "Will I get a close-up?"

"That depends on the script," Nate said.

Lance was pacing around the room on the phone once again. He hung up and turned to everyone. "That was Martin. He sends a hello. He said he's hard at work on *Death on the Quai II*.

Incredulous, everyone stared at him.

"I was just joking," Lance said.

All of a sudden, there was the sound of raindrops against the window. Ava walked over to it. The sun was shining and it was raining!

It was a sign of something and Ava couldn't wait to learn what that was.

Preview of "Death in the Louvre"

The sky over Paris was a pale shade of grey. It was a pearl grey with large swathes of pink and yellow splashed through it. The early morning June sky promised a warm sunny afternoon. For the moment, cotton-candy clouds drifted peacefully across it. The clouds moved so slowly that the sun played hide and seek with them: popping out in a glorious beam of light only to disappear behind the next fluffy mass.

When bright rays of sunshine came pouring into the Café Mollien in the Denon Wing of the Louvre Museum, Ava Sext was in heaven. Seated at an alcove table directly in front of a huge antique window that gave onto the Carrousel Garden across the road, she watched the sunlight dance on *Arc de Triomphe* at the garden's entrance. The gold leaf on its statues glittered in the bright light just as it must have two hundred years earlier when the arch was built to commemorate Napoleon Bonaparte's military victories

Like a cat basking in the sun, Ava leaned back in the warm sunshine. Two hundred years ago, who could have imagined that she -- Ava Sext, born and raised in London -- would one day be enjoying the scene over a late breakfast? And that she would be enjoying it as a Parisian...

Ava pushed her long brown hair behind her ears. Dressed in loose-fit jeans and a chic blue top by an Italian designer, she had a magenta-colored leopard print chiffon scarf jauntily wrapped around her neck, fuchsia pink sports shoes on her feet and a touch of bright red lipstick on her lips. The rest of her heart-shaped face was makeup-free. Anyone looking at her would think she was French.

"Cappuccino, a double espresso, cheesecake and an apple tart," a tall man said, setting a tray down on the table in front of her.

With a smile, Ava looked up at Henri DeAth who was looking especially dapper that morning. He was wearing dark jeans and a pale blue shirt that made his blue eyes look even bluer. A charcoal grey sweater was thrown over his shoulders. Salt and pepper hair curled around his face like a halo. In his sixties, Henri had the youngest spirit of anyone she had ever met.

Henri had been friends with Ava's late Uncle Charles. After an inheritance, Charles Sext, a New Scotland Yard detective, had quit his job and moved to France to run an outdoor bookstand on a Parisian quay overlooking the Seine River, having decided to enjoy life far from crime and criminals. However, sleuthing was in his blood. Before his death last year, he and Henri had solved several crimes together that had brought them some renown.

"A sunny day. A perfect day to visit the Louvre," Henri announced. "What tourist in his right mind would want to spend such a glorious day in a dusty museum?"

Having seen hundreds of people lined up at the pyramid entrance to the Louvre, Ava knew there were quite a few.

As Henri slid into the seat across from her, Ava, hungrier than she would like to admit, removed the items from the tray and spread them across the table.

"What do you want?" she asked, trying to keep her gaze off the apple tart that was screaming her name. The cappuccino was also calling out to her.

"Ladies' choice," Henri replied, always the gentleman.

"You go first," Ava said, hoping that he would ask for the cheesecake.

Henri raised his eyebrows. With an amused smile, he pointed at the tart and the cappuccino. Ava's heart sank.

"Those are for you. But if you prefer the cheesecake and espresso, I'll be happy to change," Henri said.

"No. I accept my fate," Ava replied with a grateful grin. She pulled the apple tart and cappuccino toward her before he changed his mind.

Henri rolled his eyes over the café's soaring ceilings, massive stone pillars and the ornate monumental staircase that led up to the café from the ground floor. "This is quite a change from Café Zola."

Café Zola was on the *Quai Malaquais* on the left bank of the Seine River in the center of Paris. Across the street from his bookstand, the café was Henri's daily coffee and lunch spot. It was a traditional café where the waiters wore long white aprons over their dark trousers and were known to be grumpy on occasion. If Ava were honest, they were grumpy on a daily basis. But that was part of Café Zola's charm.

"When are Gerard and Alain going to reopen?" Ava asked,

trying to hide the worry in her voice. Gerard and Alain were the two cousins who owned Café Zola. Gerard dealt with the customers while Alain spent his time in the café's tiny kitchen, whipping up unforgettable meals. The café had closed for works after a water leak.

"In two weeks. They've decided to renovate," Henri answered, taking a sip of his espresso.

"Renovate!" Ava repeated, horrified. "You mean modernize?" Images of neon lights and brightly-colored hip furnishings appeared before her eyes.

"Gerard and Alain? Modernize... Never. They don't even know what the word means. They're just "freshening up" the decor."

Ava furrowed her brow, not at all reassured by the term "freshening up".

Henri gestured at Café Mollien's lavish ornamentation. "This as an opportunity to spend time in the Louvre. We see it every day from our bookstands, but I can't remember the last time I was here. Until Café Zola reopens, we can have breakfast here and see some art at the same time."

"That leaves lunch," Ava said, taking a bite of her tart. It melted in her mouth. Its sweet crust contrasted perfectly with the apples' tartness.

Watching her, Henri burst out laughing. "For a skinny English girl who arrived last year, you've turned into quite the French gourmet."

"That's your fault and Alain's," Ava replied, content.

The first time Ava had gone to Café Zola, she had ordered a sandwich for lunch. Alain was so upset that he marched out of the kitchen to see what was wrong. The sandwich was quickly replaced by a *coq au vin*, rooster in wine sauce, and a *tarte tatin*, a caramelized upside-down apple tart, for dessert. It was delicious. It was also life-changing. Ava's sandwich days were behind her.

Gazing blissfully at her surroundings, Ava smiled. "I never thought I'd go to work and see the Louvre every day. In London, my office looked on a brick wall with dripping blood painted on it."

Thinking back to her career in London, Ava shuddered. A communication specialist in a boutique PR firm, her days and nights had been devoted to posting social media posts and tweeting for her celebrity clients. She realized it was time to leave when she had gone on a drunken tweeting frenzy after a romantic relationship had ended badly, and no one had noticed. In fact, some clients had even complimented her on the originality of her tweets!

Seeing the expression on her face, Henri misread her thoughts. He nodded as he bit into his cheesecake. "I agree. These pastries don't hold a candle to Alain's desserts, but we have to eat."

Ava took a sip of her cappuccino and studied the mass of humanity that was hurrying up the staircase to the Grand Gallery. People rushed by without breaking pace. Since she and Henri had arrived, the crowds coming up the stairs had grown denser.

"Where are they all going?" Ava asked, curious.

"To see the Louvre's most famous lady... the Mona Lisa. I'm

afraid the only thing they'll be able on a day like today is the head of the person in front of them. If you want to visit the Mona Lisa, you need to come on a winter evening. You'll be alone with her."

For a brief instant, Ava almost wished it were winter so she could experience that intimacy. But the sunlight streaming through the window changed her mind. It was summer. If she had her way, the beautiful weather would last forever.

"When did you last see the Mona Lisa?" Henri asked.

"I can't remember." No sooner had the words escaped her lips than a school trip to the Louvre years ago came to mind. At the time, Ava, who must have been fourteen, had been more interested in a boy called Jason than in art. She had a vague memory of standing in front of the Mona Lisa as he chatted up another girl, breaking Ava's heart.

"The Mona Lisa is a wonderful painting, but it's far from my favorite," Henri said.

"What are we seeing today?" Ava asked, taking another forkful of her apple tart. She was so ravenous, she considered picking it up with her fingers and biting into it. She refrained from doing so. Certain things were not done in France.

"13th and 14th-century Italian painting," Henri said. "We'll see works by Lorenzo Monaco, Bartolo di Fredi and Pisanello. Pisanello's portrait of the Princess of Este is enchanting." Gazing at the mass of people walking up the staircase, he shook his head. "Don't worry. We'll be far from the maddening crowd."

"I remember visiting museums on school trips. We were shepherded past painting after painting without having the chance to look at any of them. Angels and saints, sinners and sinking ships... they all blended into one big blur," Ava said, twirling her fork in the air.

Henri grinned. "I prefer sinners. Saints are never much fun."

"Uncle Charles would have agreed with you. He liked rogues and villains. I think he'd be disappointed in me."

Henri burst out laughing. "You're still young. There's plenty of time to pick up vices."

Finding his words encouraging, Ava finished her tart. "Cheesecake and apple tart aren't very French for breakfast."

"All the better. If you believed the clichés, I'd have a beret on my head, and you'd have bright pink hair. Besides, this is a late breakfast. It doesn't follow the normal Parisian breakfast rules."

Ava studied Henri as he drank his espresso. He was at home in the ostentatious gold and marble surroundings. Henri was a former French *notaire*, a notary. In France, a notary was a member of a powerful caste. They were wealthy, secretive and protective of privileges that went back hundreds of years.

Henri had once joked to Ava, "Not only do we know where the bodies are buried, we helped bury them..."

A French notary giving up his practice before he was in his dotage or dead was as rare as Christmas in August...

Impossible.

However, Henri was Christmas in August.

As well as Christmas in May, June and July...

In short, Henri was an unusual man.

He had come to Paris from Bordeaux -- a city in southwestern

France, hub of the Bordeaux wine-growing region -- to deal with a tricky inheritance. Her Uncle Charles's apartment where she now lived had sprung from that, as had the bookstands and Henri's country house in the middle of Paris.

At a mere sixty, Henri had sold his practice to his nephew and moved to Paris. Henri's former clients still appeared on a regular basis to ask him for advice. But after a long leisurely lunch at Café Zola, they would leave, reassured.

To Ava, it seemed that if anyone lived life fully, it was Henri. He truly enjoyed people. He loved food, knowledge and beauty. He had a great sense of humor and had been a true friend to her since she had moved to Paris to become a bookseller.

And after they had saved Yves Dubois, a university professor, from being murdered, she and Henri were now partners in sleuthing.

"*Sext and DeAth*. It has a nice ring to it, doesn't it?" Ava asked.

"Are you having a sign made?" Henri asked, smiling.

"Of course not. I just find it curious that you and my uncle became friends. Knowing him, he would have found the wordplay on your names extremely funny."

Henri grinned. "I agree. Charles liked the ring of *Sext and DeAth*."

Ava nodded. Henri's last name was often a source of astonishment for English speakers. DeAth was an old Flemish name. *De* meant from. *Ath* was a city in Belgium. Over time, the pronunciation of the last name had come to rhyme with the English word "death". As both her uncle and Henri possessed a wicked sense of humor, Ava suspected their last names had made their friendship inevitable.

Thinking of her uncle, Ava glanced away to hide the tears in her eyes. She owed her Paris life to him. In his will, he had left her an apartment and money. More importantly, he had left her Henri.

Looking around, Ava noticed that the café was now half-full.

When had everyone snuck in?

When she and Henri had arrived, the café had been empty.

Her Uncle Charles had often said that people miss half their lives because they don't see what's going on around them. Ava might not have missed half her life, but she had certainly missed the last ten minutes.

All at once, a shadow loomed over her.

A tall man in his late forties with wavy brown hair and blue eyes, even bluer than Henri's, was standing next to her. He seemed relieved to see her. As his eyes ran over her face, his expression changed. Confused, he looked up and peered out the window.

Startled, Ava eyed the man, waiting. French people didn't walk up to strangers unless it was urgent.

"It's a beautiful day, isn't it?" the man asked in a posh English accent.

The moment Ava heard his accent, she smiled. The man was not a desperate Frenchman. He was a fellow compatriot who had fallen under the city's spell.

"June is a lovely month to visit Paris," Henri said.

The man eyed Henri. "Do we know one another?"

"I don't believe so. I'm Henri DeAth." Henri gestured at Ava.

"My friend is Ava Sext."

The man smiled. "I'm George Starr."

"Are you here on a visit?" Henri asked in a breezy tone.

"No. I'm lucky enough to live here," George said with a grin. He turned his head to the right. Instantly, his body became rigid. Turning white, he stepped back as if warding off a blow.

Noticing the dramatic change in the man's behavior, Ava glanced around to see what had caused it. All she saw was a sea of shouting French schoolchildren being corralled through the café to the outside terrace by their teachers.

And then, like in a film, everything happened at once.

Or so it seemed to Ava.

George tilted forward and fell over the table. "Sorry. How clumsy of me," he said as he pulled himself up, clutching the chair next to her.

Before Ava could respond, George turned and sprinted out of the café, pushing his way through the rambunctious children.

Alarmed, Ava jumped up. "Henri! Something's wrong!"

Having sensed that something was off, Henri was already on his feet.

"He's headed to the stairs, Henri!" Ava shouted as she ran to the black and gold wrought iron railing that overlooked the stairway. When she reached it, there was a loud, ear-shattering scream.

The scream echoed through the café.

In horror, Ava glanced down and saw George Starr fly up in the air and go bouncing down the stone stairs. His body hit the landing with a loud thud.

For a moment, time stopped.

Everyone was silent.

No one moved.

Then sheer chaos ensued.

Screams and shouts of horror rang up from the stairwell.

Ava started to run toward the stairs. Henri held her back.

The screams and shouts were now coming from all around them. Everyone in the café leapt up and ran to the railing to see what had happened.

Feeling sick, Ava pressed her back against a stone pillar and looked down at George. His body was sprawled on the stone landing. His head was at an odd angle, and blood dripped from the back of his skull. There was no question of whether he was dead or alive.

No one could have survived a fall like that.

With a solemn look on his face, Henri turned to Ava. "I suggest we postpone our museum visit."

Frozen to the spot, Ava stared down at the body of the man who had been chatting gaily with her seconds before.

In a flash, Ava knew that the death was not an accident. For some unknown reason, George Starr had been murdered. Looking down at his lifeless body, Ava vowed to discover who the murderer was.

ABOUT THE BOOKS

Evan Hirst's *Paris Booksellers Mysteries* plunge into the joys and tribulations of living in Paris, where food, wine and crime make life worth living… along with a book or two.

Books in the series are stand-alones and can be read in any order.

Book 1: Death on the Seine
Book 2: Death in the Louvre
Book 3: Death on the Quai
Book 4: Death in Montmartre
Book 5: A Little Paris Christmas Murder
Book 6: Death at the Eiffel Tower

Evan also writes the *Isa Floris* thrillers that blend together far-flung locations, ancient secrets and fast-paced action in an intriguing mix of fact and fiction aimed at keeping you on the edge of your seat.

Books in the series are stand-alones and can be read in any order.

Book 1: The Aquarius Prophecy
Book 2: The Paradise Betrayal

Made in United States
North Haven, CT
22 October 2023

43062154R00178